Bab

SUSA

SILHOUETTE

Desire®

*All the characters in this book have no existence outside the imagination
of the author, and have no relation whatsoever to anyone bearing the
same name or names. They are not even distantly inspired by any
individual known or unknown to the author, and all the incidents are pure
invention.*

*First published in Great Britain 1997
Silhouette Books, Eton House, 18-24 Paradise Road,
Richmond, Surrey TW9 1SR*

© Susan Bova Crosby 1996

ISBN 0 373 76018 3

22-9702

*Printed and bound in Great Britain
by Mackays of Chatham PLC, Chatham*

SUSAN CROSBY

is fascinated by the special and complex communication of courtship, and so she burrows in her office to dream up warm, strong heroes and good-hearted, self-reliant heroines to satisfy her own love of happy endings.

She and her husband have two grown up sons and live in the Central Valley of California. She spent a mere seven and a half years getting through college, and finally earned a B.A. in English a few years ago. She has worked as a synchronized swimming instructor, a personnel interviewer at a toy factory, and a trucking company manager. Involved for many years behind the scenes in a local community theater, she has made only one stage appearance—as the rear end of a camel! Variety, she says, makes for more interesting novels.

Readers are welcome to write to her at P.O. Box 1836, Lodi, CA 95241, United States of America.

Other novels by Susan Crosby

Silhouette Desire®

The Mating Game
Almost a Honeymoon

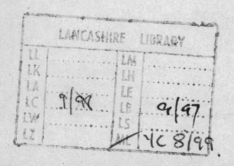

For Christine Rimmer, who is everything I admire—
talented, generous, kind, intelligent and humble. Thanks
for making the journey so much fun.

And for my wonderful editor, Melissa Jeglinski,
who wanted Patrick to have his own story.
He thanks you and so do I.

Prologue

Six thousand dollars.

The words echoed in Jasmine LeClerc's head as she pushed open the door and exited the quiet, sterile building. She descended a short flight of stairs, her legs trembling so much she had to prop herself against the discreet sign at the bottom step—Bay City Clinic, Specializing In Reproductive And Fertility Disorders.

She closed her eyes. The numbers seemed to flash in neon in front of her. Six thousand dollars.

Drawing a deep breath, she straightened, mentally tugging her dignity into place. She was stronger than this. Tougher. She had to be. Cost couldn't defeat her purpose. Not now. Not after she had come so far and had so little time remaining on her accelerating biological clock. The only viable eggs she had left were probably in wheelchairs by now, waiting to slide down a fallopian tube and on into oblivion.

She could picture them lined up at the starting gate. "Been here long?" October's egg would ask, and November's would answer, "Oh, yeah. Long time. Nigh on forty years now."

The image made her smile, her first of the day. She started walking, the mindless activity helping her focus on facts instead of emotion. The infertility counselor had said that each attempt to be artificially inseminated would cost six thousand dollars and had less than a thirty-three percent success rate.

Those weren't the numbers she'd wanted to hear.

She did some mental calculations. Her savings account could handle a couple of tries, but giving up that much money to buy herself a pregnancy meant she'd have to go back to work right after the baby was born, and she wanted to share those first precious months with her child. Plus, she really hoped to work only one job instead of the two she'd been juggling for the past seven years.

Then again, none of that mattered if neither attempt was successful.

There was another solution to her problem, of course. Her stomach knotted at the thought. She tried to block the image, but reality insisted she look at it honestly—she had to find an oblivious human donor to father her child.

She used Lamaze techniques to combat her queasy stomach, focusing on breathing patterns to relax. She was known for her honesty—brutally honest, most people called her. What she was considering required more than simple deceit. It meant outright lies. Could she actually go through with it? Could she pretend something she didn't feel? She wished she could talk to someone about it, but she didn't dare take even her sister into her confidence.

Bonk.

Something hit the backs of her knees, making her stumble a couple of steps. She caught herself before she fell, then turned around.

"Jason Alexander O'Connor. How many times have I told you not to throw that ball at people?" a woman yelled, exasperation layering each word.

Jasmine picked up the offending big blue rubber ball and smiled at the little boy with the soulful brown eyes. His mother, pushing a stroller, swooped down on him.

"That's the last time we take the ball with us." She touched Jasmine's arm. "I'm so sorry. Are you all right, ma'am?"

Jasmine winced. *Ma'am*. Another reminder of her middle age. "Yes, I'm fine. I was surprised, that's all." Crouching, she passed the ball to the boy, then shifted her glance to the stroller and the pink-bonneted baby who lay contentedly within, staring in fascination at her own tiny fists. "You have beautiful children."

"Well, one's for sale, cheap," the harried young woman said, eyeing her son. The boy turned a brilliant smile on his mother, apparently accustomed to the threat, as her mouth twitched against an answering grin. "Put the ball in the stroller, Jason, and let's go home."

Jasmine watched them walk away, the strings of her heart stretching to their limits. She shoved all concerns about dishonesty aside.

The end would justify the means, she told herself, coming to a decision. She wanted—*needed*—a baby. But first, she needed a man.

He had to be in good health, of course, and intelligent. And fertile. It would be nice if he were attractive and kind—she hadn't made love in seven years, so some tenderness and physical appeal would help settle her nerves. And he definitely had to be temporary. No dating, no relationship beyond the window of opportunity that ovulation affords . . . three days, tops.

And he could never, ever, know anything about her pregnancy. No one would ever steal a child from her again. No one.

One

———

Patrick O'Halloran paid the cabdriver, added a generous tip for the guided tour he'd been given from the San Francisco airport to his daughter's house, then stood on the sidewalk smiling at absolutely nothing.

He was in a good mood, a great mood. He was about to surprise his daughter, whom he hadn't seen since her Valentine's Day wedding a month and a half ago, and he hoped to spend a lot of time with her over the next few weeks that the doctor had ordered him to stay away from the office.

Doctors—what did they know? So, he'd had a heart attack. A *minor* heart attack, his cardiologist had reminded him at every opportunity. That didn't mean his life was over. Just because his father had died of a massive coronary at age forty-seven, and Patrick had just celebrated his forty-seventh birthday, didn't mean he would become a statistic himself.

"Dad?"

Patrick spun toward the house and grinned. "Hey, kid."

Paige O'Halloran-Warner flew down the steps and into his arms. "What are you doing here?" she asked, laughing, then squeezing him tighter. "I've missed you, Dad. Really, really missed you."

A lump formed in his throat as he hugged her back. He might have died without ever seeing her again, without seeing how happy she was. *Happy* wasn't even the word. She glowed. "I missed you, too, honey."

He didn't make eye contact with her as they moved apart. Instead he scooped up his luggage and followed her into the house, where he almost tripped over several suitcases sitting in the front entry.

"You should have called," Paige said, seeing where his gaze fell. "Rye and I are leaving in an hour for Brazil. We've got an embezzler to track down."

He refused to let his disappointment show, and he refused to tell her about the heart attack. He'd never seen her so...vibrant. Her hair bounced in springy curls, her makeup amounted to mascara and maybe a little blush. The blue jeans and cotton sweater she wore completed the casual picture. What a change from the formally dressed, perfectly made-up woman she'd been just over a month ago.

No, if he told her about his doctor's orders she would stay home with him, and he didn't want that for her.

"Patrick!"

Rye Warner hurried down the stairs. The men shook hands, then Rye retreated to Paige's side, settling his arm around her waist and pulling her snugly to him.

The gesture reminded Patrick of what was missing in his own life, and a yearning need filled him. The need for a normal existence, with a loving woman—someone to touch and hold, someone to sleep beside, someone to talk to in the deep, dark hours of the night when fear settled in and courage failed. His beautiful wife had died twenty-five years ago, leaving him with a four-year-old daughter and only a stevedore's salary to raise her on. Aside from the business he'd built, nothing and no one had replaced Priscilla in his heart. He didn't think anyone ever could. But he missed—

"Why didn't you call?" Rye asked gently, his far-too-perceptive gaze reading things Patrick wanted to keep hidden. "We have an assignment—"

"It was a spur-of-the-moment decision and I just took a chance. How long will you be gone?"

"At least a week. How long can you stay?"

They wandered into the living room and sat down.

"I was planning on getting a hotel room for a couple of weeks." Patrick watched them exchange glances. "I know what you're thinking, but everything's fine. After almost thirty years of rarely taking vacation time, I decided I was overdue. I'm letting the company take care of itself."

"I don't believe it," Paige said. "O'Halloran Shipping can't function without you there every day. At least, that's what you've always said."

Patrick rested his arms on his thighs and clasped his hands. "Well, you know, since the merger, I've had a little more freedom. I've been delegating work—"

"Are you ill, Dad?" Paige leaned toward him, forcing him to look her in the eye.

"Do I look ill?" His heart did a little dance as he waited for her answer.

"I guess not," she said finally.

His gaze shifted to Rye, who sat silently observing him. "You look good, both of you," Patrick said in an effort to distract his son-in-law. "Marriage agrees with you."

"Paige agrees with me," Rye said, twining his fingers with hers.

"I never knew it could be like this." She smiled at her husband. "He fills up every corner of my life, yet he lets me be independent, too. If anyone had told me marriage could be like this, I would have laughed at the ridiculousness of the notion.''

Patrick ached for someone to look at him with the same kind of love.

"I'm just so sorry we're leaving town now," Paige continued, her gaze returning to her father. "Promise me you won't leave before we get back. You can use our house while we're gone."

"Thanks, but I'd prefer a hotel, I think. Someplace with room service. You know my cooking skills."

A slow grin spread across Rye's face. Patrick noted it, and didn't like the pure devilment in it.

"I've got just the place." Rye stood. "Let me call and see if it's available."

"Don't go to any trouble—"

"Give up, Dad. Once he's got an idea in his head, an earthquake can't shake it loose. So, tell me everything that's happened at work since I left."

As restaurant kitchens went, it was quiet. The tinkle of utensils against china, the muffled clatter of pans on the stove, the hiss and sizzle of food cooking—sounds comforting in their familiarity. The tone of quiet efficiency pervaded the building housing the Carola, a private club whose members included the famous and the infamous, giving them space apart from paparazzi and curious onlookers.

Jasmine LeClerc hummed softly as she prepared four dinner salads. Tuesday meant a smaller crowd, a lighter load and slower pace.

"Code green, table twenty, Jazz."

Jasmine looked up at the sound of her sister's voice. Code green was staff lingo for an unaccompanied male.

"Hubba-hubba," Maggie said as she plucked at her blouse and fanned herself with the fabric, pretending to cool herself down. "And J.D. gave him to lucky ol' you."

Ignoring her sister's theatrics, Jasmine poured a healthy scoop of honey dijon dressing on each salad. She hated serving men who came to the Carola without women, although she'd gotten good at diverting their halfhearted propositions and wholehearted innuendos. Her opinion of the male species, not particularly high before she began waiting tables, had sunk to subterranean levels over the years. And the maître d', J.D., ever the hopeful romantic, took great delight in foisting single men on her, but not on the equally single Maggie—although Jasmine had her opinions about that, too.

"He looks a mite lonely to me, Jazz," Maggie said.

Hope flared briefly within Jasmine, then died. Since beginning her quest almost six months ago, she had avoided considering any club member as The Donor, as she'd come to think of him, needing the detachment and anonymity. First, most of them were married. Second, she didn't dare. No matter how desperate she became, she still needed a man who wouldn't drop back into her life.

"Men have perfected that lonely look," Jasmine said as she lifted the salad plates onto a tray, then added a basket of crusty sourdough bread and a dish of iced butter, "because women are pushovers. And as long as we allow them to behave like needy little boys, they'll continue to sucker us in."

"Pay the bank!" Maggie crowed.

Jasmine half smiled. Undoubtedly it wouldn't be her last contribution to the bank tonight. Reaching into her pocket, she withdrew a quarter and deposited it in a ceramic jar shaped like Michelangelo's David and sporting a sign on a string around its neck. She scooped up the tray and headed for the dining room. Her glance drifted to table twenty. The code green definitely qualified as hubba-hubba material. He nodded at J.D., who set a tall glass of iced liquid on the table with his usual dramatic flair. Instead of leaving immediately, J.D. stayed to talk for a few minutes.

Jasmine served salads, refilled water glasses, and tried not to look at the auburn-haired stranger who toasted the air before taking a long swallow of his drink after J.D. left. Then he opened the menu, blocking himself from her view.

He wanted a steak. A one-inch-thick prime sirloin smothered in sautéed mushrooms. He craved a huge baked potato dripping with real butter and mounded with sour cream. And chives. Chives would count as a vegetable, right?

He snapped the menu closed. He would order broiled chicken breast, steamed vegetables and rice.

It was no damn meal for a man.

Patrick glanced around the darkened dining room of the Carola. Along with hotel accommodations at a quaint ivy-covered cottage, the English countryside interior of which was a little too froufrou for Patrick's tastes, Rye had arranged a guest membership for him at an exclusive club not far from the cottage.

The scene was familiar to him—subtle background music, dark furnishings, flickering candlelight, efficient service and undoubtedly superb food, just like his club at home in Boston. Upstairs he'd probably find card rooms, a billiard room or two, and lounges, segregated by gender. He swept an encompassing glance around the room. Even the women looked the same, with their perfectly coiffed hair, their clothes hanging from their shoulders and hips in nice, straight designer lines.

His glance followed the waitress who had come into the room a few minutes earlier balancing a tray of salads on one hand. Now *there* was a woman. Generous curves in all the right places, curves that made a man wonder and dream, and maybe even salivate. As she moved around the table serving, she smiled in return to something one of the

women said and listened attentively to the man Patrick
recognized as the star of the San Francisco-based TV de-
tective series "Blue Fog." She disappeared into the
kitchen, the tail of her white-blond braid skimming her
waist. She came back empty-handed and headed toward
his booth.

"Good evening," she said, her voice intriguing in its
husky timbre. "Have you decided what you'd like tonight?"

Snared by her soft gray eyes, he focused on her face.
Late thirties, he guessed, and like the dark-haired waitress
he'd seen working the opposite side of the room, she wore
a tailored white dress shirt, narrow black tie and straight
black skirt. He looked down at the closed menu, taking
advantage of the moment to let his gaze flicker briefly to
her discreet name tag.

Jasmine. It was a rather exotic name for an American
beauty.

"I've decided," he said, handing her the menu and ordering the requisite heart-healthy meal.

"I figured you for a meat-and-potatoes man," she said,
her smile friendly.

"I guess I've eaten plenty of both in my day. But the best
way to overcome jet lag is to drink no alcohol and eat
light."

"And fresh fruit, I understand," she added. "Maybe
you'd like some for dessert?"

Patrick toasted her with his club soda, signaling an affirmative answer. Fruit. Swell. He supposed apple pie
wouldn't count.

She started to leave, then glanced sideways at him. "Do
you mind telling me— No, never mind."

"What?"

"I was being nosy, that's all. Forget it."

"Jasmine." He liked the way her name brushed his lips, bringing to mind mysterious evenings and sultry fragrances. "Ask."

"What were you toasting a while ago?"

He lifted his glass again. "A clean bill of health." He wondered at the sudden narrowing of her eyes, as if she were assessing his answer for truth.

"Was that something you were worried about?"

He sipped his drink before answering. "Not particularly. It was just my annual checkup." The lie came easily. He'd never felt so vulnerable. He just wanted it all to go away. Maybe he could learn to ignore—

"That's always a relief," she said, angling a little closer.

Curious at the change in her body language, he waited for her to make the next move.

She patted an ironed crease on the tablecloth, flattening it. "And you said you were suffering from jet lag?"

He kept his gaze on her face. "I flew in today from Boston."

"Business or pleasure?"

Patrick leaned back and smiled slightly at her show of interest. "Just a vacation."

He watched a smile flicker across her lips before she straightened.

"I'll be right back with your salad," she said.

His gaze lingered on her as she moved across the room and disappeared through a swinging door with an economy of movement, no teasing swing to her hips.

He sought a word to describe her that wouldn't get him into trouble. In his day, if you called a woman stacked or built, everyone knew what it meant. But in these days of political correctness, he was sure he couldn't use either of those words.

Missing his usual Scotch on the rocks, he sipped his club soda as visions of the gray-eyed blonde with the tempting

feminine curves filled his head. Voluptuous. Yeah, voluptuous. That suited her to a tee.

And he'd probably be slapped for even thinking it.

Jasmine set a chilled salad plate carefully on the kitchen
counter, afraid if she didn't control the movement she
would fling the plate like a Frisbee across the room.

She mentally listed his credentials. He was here on vacation, he lived three thousand miles away, and he was in
good health. Would a complete annual exam include all of
the important blood tests? she wondered. Since there
wouldn't be time to get any before they slept together—*if*
they slept together—she had to trust that it did.

He was of an age that he might be interested in her for a
brief vacation fling, instead of some twenty-year-old hard-
body he could likely have if he wanted one. A spark of interest had flared in dark green eyes that not only hadn't
undressed her with lascivious speculation, but hadn't even
looked below her chin that she could tell, except to determine her name, which put him on a pedestal as far as she
was concerned.

He wasn't wearing a wedding ring, nor did his finger
hold that telltale indentation of having recently worn one.

He was extremely attractive, with his auburn hair that
begged for a trim yet entreated a woman to comb it with
her fingers, and his tall, athletic frame looked amazingly
fit for a man she guessed was in his mid-forties.

She considered some of the other candidates she'd met
over the past six months, each of them flawed in some way.
Potential Donor 1, who she'd decided wasn't tall enough;
Donor 2, whose ears were too large; Donor 3, whose eyes
were too brooding; Donor 4, who wore turtlenecks all the
time—what had he been hiding?

She recognized the alleged flaws for the excuse they
were—to avoid making her plan a reality. But now there

was this man, who was tall enough, had perfect ears, smiling eyes and a strong, suntanned neck.

He was perfect. Too perfect. He had to have a fatal flaw. And she was going to find it.

Two

Okay, not voluptuous, Patrick decided. Too much of a political hot potato. Statuesque? He tossed that word aside, too, as Jasmine approached. The description didn't fit, either, because it implied height, and she wasn't tall, maybe just five foot five or so and, based on his experience with the opposite sex, he suspected she probably always complained about how she needed to lose ten or fifteen pounds. Not in his opinion, however.

He smiled at her as she set his salad and a basket of bread on the table.

"So, how did you end up here?" she asked, resituating the bread basket and moving the dish of butter closer to him, then shifting it again.

"Here in San Francisco or at the Carola?"

She fascinated him. She was obviously uncomfortable making small talk, seeming on the verge of running away, yet she continued to pry into his private life. He'd bet his newest fleet of cargo ships she didn't usually have personal conversations with her customers. She hadn't even introduced herself.

"Both, I guess," she said.

"My daughter lives here in the city. Her husband arranged a temporary membership at the club while I'm here."

Why did she keep doing that—smiling mysteriously over his answers, as if he was passing some kind of test?

Once again she patted the creases on the white linen tablecloth and kept her gaze lowered. "Your wife didn't come with you?"

"I'm widowed." It hurt to say the words. Even after twenty-five years it cut into him, a double-edged sword of loss and guilt.

Jasmine watched tension settle over him. Without thinking, she touched his coiled fist.

He opened his hand and captured hers, squeezing as if he were drowning and she was his lifeline. She felt the distinctive texture of calluses . . . and warmth—pure, masculine warmth. Then he released her hand and lifted his salad fork.

"Can I get you anything else? Another drink?" she asked, regretting that she'd shattered the mood with her nosiness, especially since he seemed embarrassed by his brief show of emotion. He must have lost his wife recently for his grief to be so fresh. She fought the image of taking him into her arms to hold and comfort. She understood grief. She understood it all too well.

"I'm fine, thanks," he said, dismissing her by stabbing some lettuce.

She watched him for a second, then said quietly, "I'm sorry."

He set down his fork. "It's been—"

"Hi, there, honey. My name's Magnolia. Is my sister taking good care of you?"

Jasmine watched as, in a blink, he changed moods upon the arrival of her younger sister, who was as different from Jasmine as borscht from chicken noodle soup.

"Magnolia," he repeated with some humor, glancing at Jasmine. "Your mother must've liked flowers."

"Our mama was a fine Southern belle who gave her girls respectable Louisiana names. 'Course Jazz here prefers to leave her roots behind. She treatin' you all right, is she?"

"Maggie," Jasmine cautioned, fighting a grin at her irrepressible sister.

Bright blue eyes sparkling, Maggie tossed a triumphant look in her direction then spoke conspiratorially to Patrick. "You must be one mighty interestin' man to get Jazz to carry on a conversation. She likes to keep business in its place, you understand."

Jasmine put her arm around her sister's delicate shoulders and turned her to face the opposite direction. Maggie's coal dark hair swung softly against her collar with the movement. "Table six is trying to get your attention, Magnolia, dear."

"Why, so they are!" Maggie looked over her shoulder and winked at Patrick, then left, her hips swaying provocatively.

Patrick smiled. He could handle Maggie—she wouldn't present any surprises. She knew she was flirting and so did he. His glance shifted to Jasmine. Now there was an enigma. She might be making an effort to flirt; she might not. Just the fact that she wore a conservatively loose uniform as opposed to the more formfitting one her less voluptuous sister sported said a lot about her personality—and her need to keep customers at a distance.

So why in hell was she making an effort with him?

"Don't mind my sister," Jasmine said, breaking into his thoughts.

"I like a woman who speaks her mind." Patrick held her gaze until she gave him a small smile and walked away. Ah, yes, this woman was much more interesting.

The chicken was broiled to perfection, the vegetables tender-crisp, the rice neither clumped nor sticky. It was a meal some workout guru would turn cartwheels about, but not this red-blooded American man who'd earned his calluses by moving freight. Patrick swore he could hear the last bite of chicken hit bottom in his stomach, like a bucket splashing into a well.

No way in hell was some damned plate of fruit going to fill the emptiness. Not even a basketful would do it.

His good mood deteriorated into annoyance. Hunger did that to him. As the hospital nutritionist, Nurse Crackwhip, had instructed, he visualized a healthy heart, the blood flowing unrestricted through a steadily pumping machine. Of course, she had also told him stress would add to his problems, and he was extremely stressed when he was hungry.

Eating healthy was for women.

He drummed his spoon on the table and watched Jasmine approach with his fruit plate and coffee—decaf, another curse from the evil Crackwhip. He felt the stick of pins in him at the slightest temptation to deviate from his healthy food program, as if she'd made a voodoo doll of him and would push in a pin when necessary to keep him on the straight and narrow. Okay, so it was really the road to recovery. It felt like capital punishment.

"How was your dinner?" Jasmine asked as she exchanged one plate for another, then began filling his coffee cup.

"Fine. Great."

She looked up at his tone of voice and he apologized.

"Jet lag catching up with you?" she asked, smiling.

He shrugged. It was a convenient excuse, and probably part of his problem, as well. "I'm sure a good night's rest will straighten me out. How about you? How much longer until you get off your feet?"

"A couple hours. Midnight, usually, unless we're really slow." She glanced around the room. "Excuse me. A customer wants more coffee."

Patrick jabbed a slice of cantaloupe and took a bite. Not too bad. The grapes were okay, as well. And the strawberries juicy and tasty. He felt better when he was done, and sat back to enjoy his coffee. His gaze landed on Jasmine's sister, Maggie, as she laughed with a couple of men old enough to be her father.

Hell, *he* was old enough to be her father. He'd bet she was near Paige's age, and a good ten years younger than Jasmine. Still, he was holding together all right, considering he had an almost-thirty-year-old daughter. The first strands of gray had made their appearance over the past year but his hairline hadn't receded at all.

And recently he'd been more sought after than ever. The reason for his sudden popularity probably stemmed from the announcement a few months ago of the merger of his company, O'Halloran Shipping, with the smaller firm of Collins-Abrahamson, especially since actual dollar figures had been revealed in newspaper articles. When his net worth had become public knowledge, ambitious mamas had doubled their dinner party invitations and seated him next to their twenty-something daughters, hoping to draw his interest.

There was nothing wrong with either his eyesight or his libido. He found many of those young women beautiful, sexy... and far too young to be of interest. He wanted a woman who had a memory of the Vietnam War, not one who'd learned about it in high school history class. Neither did he want a woman who hung on his every word or whose focus was on shopping and partying.

Then there were the divorced women blatantly prowling for a new mate . . . and meal ticket.

Why couldn't he find someone in between, maybe someone with a couple of children he could still be a father to? He wiped a hand down his face. Nothing like acknowledging your mortality to bring on an attack of sentimentalism, he decided.

"All done?" Jasmine asked. "Or would you like more coffee?"

He hadn't even heard her come to the table. "I've had enough, thanks."

"Are you running a tab or paying cash?"

"I don't know how long I'll be around, so I don't want to run a tab."

"Oh? This is a really quick trip, then?"

"I'm not sure. My daughter and son-in-law had to leave town. As soon as they get back I'll probably be with them instead of coming here."

She placed his check upside down on the table. "So, you may not be back?" she asked, her voice soft but her chin lifted.

Patrick didn't know what to make of the contradictions he saw in her. She looked as if she'd had the wind knocked out of her and seemed suddenly small and lost, yet she also appeared ready to do battle. "Do you want me to come back, Jasmine?" he asked, equally softly and with as much intensity.

"I—I've enjoyed talking with you."

"Do you want me to come back?" He had a sudden urge to kiss away her hesitation, and an even stronger urge to feel her pressed against him. Was she stalling because she was an employee and he a guest? Or because she was feeling the same attraction that he was, and didn't know how to handle it either, especially this soon? She was the first woman he'd met in a long time whose intentions weren't conspicuously apparent within the first fifteen minutes of acquaintance—which didn't say much about his choice of women lately.

"Good night," she said softly.

Patrick watched her walk determinedly away, then he pulled a slim gold pen from inside his jacket and wrote a message on the check stub. After adding several bills, he strode out of the club and into the night.

Jasmine watched him leave, regretting that she hadn't answered him. She didn't have time to be a fatalist. If she wanted something to happen, she had to make it happen.

She'd seen him write something on the check. Usually when a man did that, it was his phone number. Please, don't let it be his phone number, she prayed. She wanted him to be better than that.

First she noticed the staggering tip he'd left, then she lifted the check. "I'll be back." The words were printed in bold, masculine script.

She closed her eyes, tore off the perforated stub and shoved it into her pocket, keeping her hand on it for a few seconds. She'd seen complexity and intelligence in the man, along with some pain and, she was pretty sure, mutual attraction.

She hoped he would be the one to fath—be The Donor, yet she didn't even know his name.

And she didn't dare ask J.D., who would gloat over finally accomplishing his goal of the past year—getting her to show the slightest interest in a man.

No, she had to wait for him to come back and then work up her nerve to entice him to her bed. It was a tall order for a man-hating woman who treasured honesty above all else.

Honesty. Why should she worry about it? How long had it been since a man had been completely honest with her?

Her father had left before her first birthday. Her first stepfather lasted six months. Her second stepfather had stuck it out until Maggie was almost three.

Then there was Jasmine's ex-husband, Deacon, the supposed love of her life. He'd broken through all of her defenses and convinced her to marry him. She'd given up so much of herself to please him. But when he'd wanted out, she'd suddenly become a second-class citizen—and her children, Matthew and Raine, pawns in his game.

Six years ago he'd spirited their children out of the country. Six years of her searching and hoping. Six years of hell. What would it be like to have so much money and power that you could break all the rules, legal and moral? she wondered for the thousandth time, even as her subconscious whispered that she was breaking the rules by deciding to find a donor—not a father. No. She couldn't give in to that particular weakness. The end had to justify the means. For once, her needs were going to come first.

"What's going on between you and the code green from last night?" Maggie asked as she and Jasmine changed into their uniforms in the women's locker room.

"Nothing." Jasmine almost wished for a more figure-hugging uniform like her sister's, something to draw the man's interest in a hurry. The basal thermometer had registered a normal temperature that morning, but she had to be ovulating soon.

"Uh-huh," her sister commented as she lined her lips with cherry red lipstick.

"Has anyone ever told you that you look like Snow White?" It was an old joke between them. Jasmine with her long blond hair had always been Sleeping Beauty. They taunted each other with the contrast whenever they wanted to change the subject.

Maggie sighed. "Why is it we complain about wanting men to admire us for our minds, then we spend a fortune on makeup?" She turned toward her sister. "You're as transparent as spun sugar, you know. Not only did you spend time talking to that gorgeous hunk of masculinity, you only had to put one quarter in the jar the whole evening and *that* was before you met him.''

''So?'' Jasmine leaned into her locker to exchange shoes.

''So... you're good for three or four slams against the male gender every night. How am I supposed to buy myself a wedding dress if you stop maligning men? I've only saved two hundred and sixty-two dollars so far. I'm counting on you.''

Jasmine tossed her street shoes into the locker. ''You might find it handy to get yourself a fiancé first.''

''By my thirtieth birthday I—''

''Better hurry up.'' Jasmine shut the door and gave the combination lock a twirl.

Maggie sniffed at the reminder. ''Obviously, you don't want to discuss your gentleman caller.''

''There's nothing to say. He came, he ordered, he left. Same as a thousand other men before him.''

''Except you didn't have conversations with the other nine hundred and ninety-nine.'' Maggie pushed open the door and preceded Jasmine down the hall and into the kitchen.

''Only one out of a thousand men is worth engaging in conversation.''

Maggie pointed dramatically at the Michelangelo jar labeled Men Are The Scum Of The Earth, with its handprinted addendum, Except J.D. ''Two hundred and sixty-two dollars *and* twenty-five cents.''

Compact. Patrick had finally come up with a word to describe Jasmine that wouldn't get him into trouble. Maybe. She probably wouldn't think it much of a compliment.

He'd spent the day contemplating her behavior. She hadn't wanted to be interested in him, yet she was. She hadn't flaunted herself before him, yet he'd been more attracted than he'd been in years to any woman. He hadn't let her catch him eyeing her—he'd learned that women either loved or hated that kind of attention—but he'd observed her thoroughly.

As he followed the maître d', a dark-haired man by the name of J. D. Duran, to the same table as the previous night, Patrick realized he was nervous. That in itself was a rarity. He'd always had an abundance of self-confidence. Suddenly he felt like a teenager at his first school dance, and he didn't know any of the steps.

He'd just been served his club soda when Jasmine made her way to his table.

"So. Your daughter isn't back yet," she said, looking at his glass.

"I made you a promise."

She lifted her gaze. "I didn't know whether to believe you."

"Now you know." He said the words lightly, not wanting the conversation to get too serious, and he was rewarded by seeing her shoulders relax.

"Still recovering from jet lag?" she asked. "Club soda again?"

"Drinking alone is a sobering thought." Nurse Crackwhip could keep her stickpins to herself, too, he thought. "I slept twelve hours straight last night. I guess I needed this vacation more than I realized."

"How'd you spend your day?"

He grinned. "Doing something I haven't done in years. Watching television."

"San Francisco is a beautiful city. You should get out and see it."

"If I had a companion—"

"Well, hello again, honey."

"Miss Magnolia," Patrick drawled, shifting his glance to the dark-haired woman.

"Did you come back for more of our tasty morsels?"

The ambiguous words made Patrick smile. "My appetite's healthy." His gaze flickered to Jasmine, who was watching her sister indulgently.

Maggie eyed his suit jacket. "It appears you favor Italian tailors."

"Not unless Geoffrey St. Clair has stopped telling the world he's the only important African-American designer."

"Really? It's a St. Clair?"

Patrick leaned forward. "I knew him when he was Jeff Troutner. He gives me suits to buy my silence." He laughed at the expression on Maggie's face. "I'm kidding. Well, not about his name, but that's common knowledge. He and my daughter went to school together from kindergarten on."

Jasmine let them talk for a minute as she looked him over, noting more detail this time. His hair was a little long but well cut, his clothing already noted as designer. When he showed Maggie the trademark St. Clair logo embroidered in the lining of the jacket, Jasmine spotted a discreet monogram on the stark white dress shirt, which was probably made of the finest cotton known to man.

What had she been thinking? She couldn't intentionally deceive this man. He was a power unto himself, she could see that now. He probably headed up some high-revenue computer company or high-visibility law firm. He wouldn't be welcomed at the Carola unless he had money and power to back him, no matter who his son-in-law was.

What in the world would he want with *her*—some waitress who saved fifty percent of her income in the useless hope that she could have a second chance at mother-hood? He probably made in a month what had taken her seven years to save. He was so far out of her league, they weren't even playing the same sport. She'd already played a mismatched game once in her life. And lost.

You only need him for a day, maybe two. The reminder slithered from her conscience to her brain, her practical side emerging to tamp down the emotional side. It only mattered that he be attracted for a couple of hours, maybe two nights in a row. Then he'd have his visit with his daughter and return to his life in Boston. Surely a couple of nights in bed together would satisfy his curiosity about her. He might even pick up on the fact she was faking it with him and not want a repeat performance.

And maybe she would end up with a child from their brief affair. But perhaps she could give him something, too—the human contact missing in his life since his wife died.

That was the way to look at the situation, of course. A brief, life-altering bisecting of lives, then each could move on. No broken hearts, just a moment out of time.

"Jasmine." Patrick watched her seem to shake herself back into the real world. Maggie had left half a minute ago, yet Jasmine had stayed frozen in place, her eyes glazed.

"I'm sorry," she said with a slight smile. "Are you ready to order?"

She angled toward him and tossed her head, a gesture he would expect her sister would make. Every time he decided Jasmine was just being friendly, she would do something obviously flirtatious—and look uncomfortable doing so.

On her recommendation he ordered the fresh fish of the day, his mouth watering for the steak he'd watched her place in front of another customer just before she'd come

to his table, but Crackwhip's pin jabbed him just as he'd
been about to order. He slid out of his jacket and started
to lay it across the seat beside him.

She reached for it. "I'll hang that up for you, sir."

"Patrick," he said. "Patrick O'Halloran."

"Mr. O'Halloran."

"Patrick."

Three

___

Patrick O'Halloran. Her baby would have an Irish father. And maybe his beautiful auburn hair and all that emotion she could see in his eyes.

Jasmine accepted the jacket and took a step back. "I'll bring your salad," she said, then walked to the coat check cubicle, trying to control her reaction. For the first time, genuine hope filled her.

Looking around and finding herself alone, she cautiously lifted the jacket to her face and breathed in the distinctly male fragrance that lingered there...and the warmth. The temptation to slide the jacket on and hug herself was overwhelming. She, Jasmine LeClerc, co-founder of Man-Haters Anonymous, wanted to wallow in this man, Patrick O'Halloran, who she'd bet her last dollar made love with a slow hand and hot need.

What would his hands feel like on her skin? Would he kiss her for a long time or would he rush through that part

of lovemaking? Would he insist she take the lead sometimes or would he want to be the one in charge all the time?

Jasmine, you idiot. She hung up his coat, slid a receipt
over the hanger and pulled off the stub to give to him.
What was she thinking? Even if he was interested, she
couldn't do anything about it tonight. She had to wait until she stood a chance of becoming pregnant. Which meant
trying to keep him interested enough to come back, but
without seeming like a tease until the time was right. She
didn't know if she could walk that tightrope.

Patrick watched her set his salad and bread on the table
then lay the coat check stub beside the salt and pepper
shakers.

"I'll get that for you when you're ready. Do you need
anything else?" she asked.

"No, thanks." *Except maybe a Scotch on the rocks, a
slab of prime rib, a big bed and you.* Ah, yes, all of his
cravings satisfied at once, everything that had been denied him since the little medical problem. That would be a
perfect night, he decided as he watched her move away
from him.

He bided his time through the evening, waiting for the
right moment to ask her out, wondering whether she would
be willing to go somewhere tonight or if he'd have to wait
until tomorrow. Chafing at the confinement of the booth,
he made himself linger over his third cup of coffee.

He looked at his watch for the fifth time in forty-five
minutes. Still more than an hour to go until she would get
off work, but he didn't think he could consume another
drop of anything liquid. He could stall a few more minutes by going to the rest room. Then he would just ask her.

What did he have to lose? If she said yes, great. If she
turned him down, that would be the end of that. He was
ready for a livelier environment anyway. The peace and
quiet of the Carola was getting on his nerves, adding to his

stress, especially sitting at the booth for hours on end. Although he'd also found something enlightening about being alone and trapped—he could observe. Which was why he'd noticed that J.D. and Maggie spent a lot of time casting surreptitious glances at each other. The tall, broad-shouldered J.D. kept a close watch on the flirtatious and sassy Maggie, who sashayed a little more wickedly when the man was nearby.

Shaking his head and smiling, Patrick started to stand when Maggie strolled up.

"If you want Jazz to go out with you, honey, you can't take no for an answer."

He took his seat again. "I take it she doesn't date much."

"An understatement." Maggie glanced around, apparently checking on Jasmine's whereabouts. "Look, honey, she's interested. I can tell you that. But if you intend on toying with her affections, I would strongly advise you to *take* no for an answer. Frankly, I believe she could use a good time or two, but only if she knows up front this is temporary."

"How could I promise anything else? We don't know each other."

"We've all seen *Pretty Woman,* honey, where the poor girl from the wrong side of the tracks makes the rich man throw caution to the wind, no matter what the public's opinion might be. It was just a modern-day fairy tale, and women like Jazz and me know it. So treat her with fairness. That's all I ask."

"I give you my word."

She nodded. "You have kind eyes."

Did he? While he'd never been accused of mistreating anyone, he didn't think there was a well of kindness in him beyond the average. Maybe the heart attack was changing him more than he thought. Then again, maybe it was just Jasmine.

Now or never, he decided, taking a deep breath as Maggie hurried away when she spotted Jasmine marching to his table. Taking care of business first, he asked for his bill and handed her the coat check stub, deflecting whatever emotions seemed anxious to spill out of her. By the time she returned with his jacket, he'd paid the bill, and she seemed calmer. But the sparks he'd seen intrigued him more than her pretense of flirting.

He stood as she arrived, and she held up the jacket, indicating he should turn around. He couldn't remember anyone doing that for him, ever, and he was uncomfortable letting her. Then he felt her fingertips graze his neck as she straightened the collar before brushing her hands across his shoulders, patting the fabric in place, a wifely gesture that startled him into stillness.

When he could manage it, he turned around. "I'd like to take you out when you get off work. You know the city, so you could choose where."

Her gaze settled chest-level on him. "Thank you for the invitation, but I'm exhausted."

"Tomorrow, then? During the day? Breakfast or lunch? You name the time and place."

Her eyes flickered briefly to his face, then lowered again. "I'm sorry. I can't tomorrow."

He bent down a little, keeping his voice low. "Have I misinterpreted?"

Jasmine held herself still. His breath was warm against her forehead. She could lean forward two inches and be able to rest her head against his shoulder. "Misinterpreted?"

"Your interest?"

Anticipation surged through her. Misinterpreted? Not likely. But she couldn't tell him that, not tonight. She wanted—*needed*—him to come back tomorrow and maybe the next and the next, until she was ovulating. "I'm just saying no for now."

"So if I ask tomorrow, I might get a different answer?"

"Maybe." She should smile at him, flirt with him, something. But she couldn't even look him in the eye. The lies would show.

He was quiet for too long. She finally looked up.

"I won't promise, but I'll try," he said.

"I hope you do," she answered quietly, giving him a smile of sorts. "If not for dinner, maybe you'd enjoy a card game or two upstairs. I'm sure you could find a table to join."

"Good night, Jasmine."

"Good night."

He waited, just staring at her.

"Patrick," she added. "Good night, Patrick." *Come back tomorrow, please,* she begged him silently as he walked away.

"I don't mind you talking to him when I'm there, but I don't trust you alone with him," Jasmine said in clipped tones as she cornered Maggie in the hallway a few minutes later.

Maggie's eyes opened wide. "I wasn't trying to lure him. I wouldn't do that to you, Jazz. You know that."

"I'm just telling you I don't need your help where he's concerned."

"Help? We were just shooting the breeze. Honest."

Jasmine wished she could take her sister into her confidence, but she knew Maggie would go crazy if she knew. Jasmine had never known anyone who so totally believed in the sacred order of things the way Maggie did. Dating, marriage, *then* children. Well, Jasmine had tried that once. It had been enough.

But if Maggie knew Jasmine had every intention of seducing that glorious man solely for the purpose of having his child, not only would she interfere, she would probably even tell Patrick. *Patrick*. Even the name made her shiver with anticipation.

"Shooting the breeze? I don't believe you," Jasmine said. "You know how I feel about men. I have good reason to feel nothing but contempt. One seemingly nice man isn't going to change my opinion of the gender."

"Jazz—"

"I mean it, Maggie. Don't interfere with—"

Maggie's hand landed against Jasmine's mouth. "Hush."

The hairs on the back of Jasmine's neck stood up. Even without confirmation, she knew Patrick had come up behind her. He must have gone to the rest room before he left. She'd been vaguely conscious of the door opening, but she hadn't tempered her speech. *Please let us have an earthquake right now,* she prayed uselessly.

"You're going to pay for this one with more than quarters," Maggie whispered to her before disappearing.

Steeling herself, Jasmine turned around. Had he heard her words to Maggie?

"Good night again," he said as he started to move past her in the narrow confines of the hallway, brushing against her and smiling.

Relieved, she concentrated on the sensation of his body skimming hers, then he stopped, pressed her against the wall and kissed her. Not a hard, quick kiss but a gentle merging of lips and breath, a kiss meant to entice. A kiss that started at their mouths but flowed the way of hot, thick, maple syrup over pancakes, down, around and through her body, saturating her with sweetness and temptation.

He settled his hands at her waist; hers glided up his chest. He slid his hands over her rear and pulled her closer; hers slipped behind his back to curve over his shoulder blades, bringing their chests as close as their hips. His tongue swept her lips then dipped inside her mouth. Was that sound coming from her? God, he was so warm, so very warm.

He lifted his head and stood in silence until she opened her eyes. She saw that his smile was gone, replaced with an intense expression she could put no name to.

"What you have to understand, Jasmine, is that *seemingly* is your operative word. A man can be seemingly nice. Then again, he may be an expert at pulling the wool over the eyes of unsuspecting women. It's probably better that you continue to feel contempt for all men than to trust any of us individually. You might end up lonely as hell, but you'll find comfort in the knowledge you're right, I'm sure."

He strode away from her as she wilted against the wall and closed her eyes, blocking her final glimpse of him.

She wouldn't look, not yet, Jasmine decided as she continued serving the party of eight. From the corner of her eye she could see J.D. leading a single customer to a booth in her section, the same booth where Patrick had sat the previous two nights. Patrick, who had given her hope before her foolish words had sounded a death knell to her dream, mournfully, dolorously, plaintively.

Yet a small part of her still clung to a fragment of hope that he was a man who didn't give up easily.

She held her breath as she tucked her tray under one arm and casually, almost carelessly, glanced at the lone man . . . with the fringe of shockingly white hair.

I am not going to cry. Again and again she repeated the order as she slipped into the kitchen and busied herself by slicing bread and building two salads.

"Why'd you put ten dollars in the jar?" Maggie asked, coming up beside her. She leaned a hip against the stainless-steel counter. "Crime and punishment?"

"It was the tip he left last night. I couldn't keep it, so you might as well add it to your dress fund."

"He really got to you, didn't he, Jazz? In a way that no man has, not in a long time."

Jasmine scooped dressing on the salad. "You'd think I would have learned with Deacon, wouldn't you?"

Maggie made a crude noise. "You can't compare Deacon with anyone."

"Rich is rich. Power is power. I'm not blaming Patrick, you understand. It was my fault entirely. But I was foolish to think for even a minute a man like that might want me. In the end, I'm glad he overheard. Better to kill the possibilities now than later, I think."

"But some part of you wants the fairy tale."

"I'm human," Jasmine said, forcing the words past a lump burning her throat. "But if I really do want to have a relationship with a man again, I need to look at my own kind. Someone from the diner, instead of here."

Maggie raised her brows. "From the sublime to the ridiculous. The people you meet at that afternoon job of yours swing to the other side of the pendulum, don't you think? And since when did you start defining yourself by your job? You're smart, you're beautiful, and any man would be lucky to have you, especially your Patrick-the-gorgeous-hunk-of-masculinity."

Jasmine hugged her sister. "Have I told you lately how much I love you? For all that I resented Mom getting married again and having a baby when I was ten, you were the best thing that happened in my life." She stepped back and moved to the sink to wash her hands.

"What's weighing on you, Jazz?" Maggie asked softly, following her. "I can't remember seeing you this emotional since—"

Jasmine let out a shaky laugh. "Don't mind me. I'm ovulating."

"You mean, PMS'ing."

Jasmine shrugged, then lifted the salads onto her tray, choosing to forget her problems by working harder than usual. She kept up a constant dialogue with customers, drawing Maggie's curious looks as she laughed, sometimes a little too boisterously. She would not cower. She would not grieve. She would continue to be strong and independent and—

Oh, God, and *childless.*

Midnight came. She changed into a sweater, jeans and tennis shoes for the walk home. Usually J.D. played bodyguard, but he had a late date. The problem with living only four blocks from work was that it was too close to justify a cab ride, and waiting at a bus stop seemed more dangerous than walking.

She stepped out into the night and glanced at the sky, sensing imminent rain. In a way she welcomed it, because it kept some of the crazies off the street. She could make a dash for home without looking around every bend and within every doorway. Cursing her all-day distraction, which had resulted in her forgetting her windbreaker, she folded her arms across her stomach, put her head down and began walking against the wind.

Up the concrete walkway she hurried, then out the gate with its discreet wrought-iron *C,* identifying the club to its members. She latched the gate and turned in the direction of her apartment. A man blocked her path. Knowing instinctively who stood there, she slowly lifted her gaze, taking in the look-alike wardrobe of sweater and jeans. His expression broadcasted his reluctance to be there, as did his words.

"I tried to stay away."

Four

———

Patrick lifted a hand to her cheek and felt her shiver from the touch of his icy skin. He'd been waiting for almost an hour. Perhaps *waiting* wasn't the right word. He'd walked past the building then returned three times, not wanting to see her, not being able to keep his distance.

"Jasmine." Her name sound magical and mysterious to him, conjuring up visions he should probably ignore. "Did you mean what you said last night?"

She looked away from him and sighed. "Yes and no."

"Meaning?" Somehow her hands had settled within his and her warmth radiated to him.

"What I said to Maggie was just automatic reaction. It didn't really pertain to you in particular."

"You've been hurt before."

"Haven't we all?"

"But you more than most, I think."

She shrugged one shoulder, and he focused on their

joined hands, feeling her anticipation as she waited to learn what he wanted from her.

"I'm not making any promises—"

"I don't want promises, Patrick."

"I just want to spend some time with you. You can't imagine the loneliness." *The nights are long and scary,* he wanted to tell her. *I lie awake listening to my heartbeat, and sometimes it feels like it stops.*

"Yes, I can," she whispered. "Oh, yes, I can."

He heard it in her voice, too—loss and longing. "Night Flower," he said softly, "will you spend an hour with me?"

She rubbed the bridge of her nose in a nervous gesture. "I could use some warming up."

He leaned a little to block the rain from her face as it began to fall. The wind howled. "What's open around here where we could get coffee?"

"Do you have a coffee maker in your hotel room?"

Surprised, he focused his gaze intently on her. "Yes," he answered slowly. "And a fireplace. Two, as a matter of fact."

"Sounds good to me."

If it hadn't been pouring he would have made her be specific about what she expected of him. But first he needed to get them out of the rain.

They ran the short distance, splashing through pot-holes of trapped water that was accumulating quickly in the deluge. He tugged her around a three-story house that had been converted into a hotel, then followed a pathway until they ended up at a brick cottage nestled in an Eden-like garden of greenery behind the building.

"Quick," he said, urging her forward with a hand at her lower back as he unlocked the door.

"I can't go inside like this!" Jasmine pressed herself against the building, under a short overhang, as he swung open the door.

"Why not?"

"I'll get everything soaked. So will you."

"People will clean it up."

The patient exasperation in his voice made her smile. "Men. You know, if you had to do the cleaning, you wouldn't be so blasé." She glanced inside. "Go get some towels from housekeeping."

"At this hour?"

"Oh. I hadn't thought about the time. Well, I guess—"

Patrick swept her into his arms and carried her over the threshold, then kicked the door shut. He walked directly into the bathroom and set her in the claw-footed tub. "Take off your shoes. I'll get towels."

"Take yours off, too," she said, grabbing his arm. "You're squishing water out with every step."

They sat on the rim of the tub and each pulled off soaked leather sneakers. The intimacy of the act struck Jasmine as soon as they both set their bare feet flat in the tub and looked at each other.

"Do you want to take a hot shower?" he asked finally.

"Okay."

He sat up a little straighter. After a few seconds he climbed out and grabbed the hotel-provided, navy blue velour bathrobe, laying it within arm's reach of the tub. "You don't need to lock the door behind me," he said carefully. "I won't come in."

Why, he's nervous, Jasmine realized, more nervous than she was. The thought relaxed her. She smiled. "I trust you."

He nodded. "I'll fix something to warm us. I've got coffee and tea, or—"

"You."

His head jerked back a little and his nostrils flared. "Me." Not a question, but a statement of controlled surprise.

Jasmine stood and moved close to him. She lifted her hands to brush back his wet hair, not daring to look at his face until she thought she could actually get words out. She settled her hands at the back of his neck, letting her thumbs brush his skin from his ears to the base of his throat. "I haven't made love in seven years." If his pulse hadn't started pounding in the neck veins beneath her fingers, she never would have known how her words affected him. She tried not to smile. "I'd like to end the drought."

"With me?"

She laughed. "No, with the president."

"It's just... You don't know me."

"I know what I need to know, and I'm afraid if I wait, there won't be a chance at all. Am I right?"

"Maybe."

"You probably don't like forward women," she said as she pressed her lips to his throat. "You probably like being the one who initiates everything—"

"No." *Ba-boom.* Patrick's heart announced its reaction. *Ba-boom. Ba-boom.* The sound vibrated in his chest and echoed in his ears. He took a deep breath. Her rain-soaked hair smelled of strawberries, inundating him with anticipation of the sweetest dessert in his memory. "Your full participation is welcome," he said finally, putting his arms around her as she laid her head against his shoulder. "But I can't help wondering, why me? Why now?"

"Why not you? Why not now?"

Ba-boom. Her arm snaked around his waist and glided under his sweater to stroke his damp skin. *Ba-boom.* He clamped his hands on her elbows, pushing her back a little. "I don't have protection," he said.

"You don't need any."

He searched her face, seeking answers she either didn't have or didn't want to give. "I'm forty-seven years old. I don't have any desire to become a father at this age."

"I should have phrased it differently," she said, calmly meeting his gaze. "You don't have to worry about my getting pregnant. I'm no spring chicken, either. I'm not going to trap you. I just want to be with you."

"And when I go home?"

"I know you live a life totally different from mine. You belong with your own. I belong with mine. That's it."

"But for now—"

"For now, we can ease the loneliness for each other."

Because he couldn't wait another minute, he kissed her, softly, briefly. *Ba-boom*. "I'll be waiting," he said, then turned to leave.

"Patrick?"

He faced her and saw shyness as she twisted her hands together, an action distinctly at odds with her boldness of just a minute ago. "I have just one favor to ask."

"What's that?"

"Could you, just for tonight, pretend you love me? Just a little?"

Ba-boom. *Ba-boom*. He hadn't loved a woman in twenty-five years, not since Priscilla. She had died because he'd gotten her pregnant again when the doctor had said she might not survive another pregnancy. "I'm not a monster, Jasmine. I'll treat you with respect."

Jasmine closed her eyes for a moment, waiting for lightning to strike her at her half-truths. But all she felt was a sense of rightness. She wanted her baby created in a loving moment, if not out of love. It was important that he or she be conceived in a night of beauty, not just physical pleasure. She looked at him, the man she had chosen to father her child. He was a good man, and strong. A kind man who didn't deserve to be lied to. But didn't she deserve something, too?

His silence unnerved her. She almost told him to forget it—she didn't need this extra tension.

"This is the honeymoon cottage," he said at last.

Hope filled her again. "Is it?"

"My son-in-law arranged the room. He told me he hoped I enjoyed my visit as much as he had."

"What does that mean?"

"He and my daughter—" He looked around, obviously uncomfortable with the sudden thought. "They were here."

"For their honeymoon?"

"They didn't wait that long."

Jasmine smiled. She liked that he was protective of his daughter, even though she was an adult. "You've already carried me over the threshold, but it would just be pretend for us, Patrick."

He stared at her for so long she felt mesmerized. Then he walked toward her, his gaze on hers, and stepped into the tub. He grasped the hem of her sweater and pulled it over and off her. She was grateful that she'd worn her only remotely sexy bra and panties, ones she hadn't worn in years. But she'd been hopeful tonight—

Her zipper grated all the way down, echoing in the tiled room. She stepped out of the soft denim as he bent to help. When he straightened and looked at her, she saw tension settle in his face, hardening his jaw, flaring his nostrils. She hadn't been undressed by a man in years and years. Maybe not since her honeymoon so long ago. She had forgotten the thrill of anticipation as each garment was peeled away to reveal flesh and vulnerability. Cool air and hot breath flowed over her sensitized skin; pinpricks of response stabbed at her. Her body swelled with need, her nipples tightened into painful knots. *Touch me. Please touch me.*

Her silent plea went unanswered for endless seconds, then a tremor raced through her as he reached behind her and unfastened her bra. His gaze never left hers as he pulled off the lacy fabric and draped it over the tub with her clothes. Still watching her face, he hooked his thumbs into her panties and pushed, kneeling as they slid down to her ankles. Gathering them as she lifted each foot, he carefully set them atop her clothes.

She expected him to rise, but he stayed there, as if needing to catch his breath. Suddenly he pressed his face against her stomach and cupped her rear in his large hands, holding her to him, his breath dusting her tender flesh with heat and harshness, his emotions spilling out. She started to shake with the wonder of it all. He was everything she could have hoped for, and more. And he needed her. He needed her as much as she needed him, even if for different reasons.

Or were they? Maybe she needed more from him than a child. Maybe she really needed the rest of what he could give her.

No. She couldn't think like that. History could not get a chance to repeat.

"Patrick," she said quietly as she brushed his hair with her hands, fighting holding him closer, afraid of getting lost in what he could offer.

"You're shivering." He stood, then made no attempt to hide his perusal of her, although his hands were clenched into fists at his sides. "And you're wrong," he said, smiling at her as she twitched uncomfortably at the inch-by-inch scrutiny.

"About what?"

"There's a lot of spring left in you, chicken. Ruffling your feathers should be fun."

He was good at that, creating then relieving tension. She watched him shut the door behind him before she turned on the water, thinking what a lucky woman his wife had been.

Patrick prowled the living room. He'd started a fire there as well as in the bedroom and had draped her clothes across a couple of chairs he'd set near the hearth, then he'd changed into dry jeans and a T-shirt, leaving his feet bare.

The shower was still running. Either she was stalling or she was shampooing her long hair. He wished he'd made love to her in the bathtub when he'd had the chance. He'd never liked planned, sanitized sex, preferring instead a spontaneous moment, and a woman who smelled like herself, not soap. He knew that women felt differently about it, however, and he allowed that they were more willing participants when they felt comfortable with themselves and the situation.

So, Jasmine would feel better if she showered, and he had needed a few minutes alone, as well. While he'd knelt in front of her in the tub, the thumping in his chest had intensified beyond the noticeable increase in tempo when he'd run home with her, beyond when he'd carried her into the room. He'd been glad to have a moment or two alone. And in just a few minutes he was going to have complete access to her body. Her perfect, incredible body. *Ba-boom.*

He wanted his heart to stop doing that, reminding him how fragile it was. This whole situation was awkward enough without mortality echoing in his ears. When he'd asked the cardiologist about sex, his advice—"Only with your wife. You shouldn't get *too* excited"—had been given with a smile.

"But I'm not married," Patrick had responded.

The doctor had shaken his head seriously. "Then I guess you're outta luck."

"For how long?"

The doctor laughed. "That's an old joke, Patrick. You can have sex whenever you feel ready."

"How do I know when I'm ready?"

"Listen to your body. You'll know."

Listen to my body. Right. My body keeps giving me mixed signals.

Then there was the issue of birth control. After Priscilla died, it had been years before he could sleep with another woman. Instead he'd spent his time building his company and raising his daughter. Guilt had burrowed into him and stayed, along with the love that had never really diminished through the years. He should have had a vasectomy instead of relying on other methods so that Priscilla wouldn't get pregnant, but she wouldn't let him do it. They'd behaved so irresponsibly. And they'd both paid the price.

So he'd never gotten around to having a vasectomy, then by the time he was ready for any kind of relationship again, there were other things to consider, diseases as well as pregnancy, making a vasectomy superfluous. He'd been a careful man all these years.

Could he believe Jasmine? Was she telling the truth about herself?

The shower stopped. *Ba-boom.* He grabbed a couple of pillows from the bed and tossed them on the couch in front of the living room fire. They'd start there and go slowly. Pretend he loved her? He didn't know how effectively he could do that, but he could make the moment last, and he could make it memorable. In a way, this was the first time he'd made love, too, since his life had begun anew. He would appreciate it more, savor the moment, treasure the memory.

The bathroom door opened; the light snapped off. He watched her step into the living room, lit only by the crackling fire and one small mantel light.

Her hair still hung in one braid down her back. Even bundled in the blue robe, she looked damp and dewy and rosy and . . . apprehensive.

"Did you change your mind?" he asked, walking toward her.

Five

Jasmine jumped, startled. She hadn't seen him standing beyond the hearth. Her gaze settled on him as he approached. "What if I had?"

"I'd walk you home."

"That simple?"

"Or order pizza for us. Your choice."

He stood in front of her, not attempting to touch her, his eyes smiling.

She smiled back. "A less secure woman might think you found her less than irresistible, to give up so easily."

"But not you."

"I have my insecurities."

"I want you, Night Flower, on whatever terms. Have no doubt about that."

Night Flower. She'd always hated being compared to a flower, but he made her sound mysterious. "I haven't changed my mind, Patrick."

"Good," he said, trailing his fingers across her cheek, along her jaw, down her arm. He captured her hand in his and backed up, pulling her toward the couch. "There's no reason to hurry, though. Let's sit by the fire for a while. Are you sure you don't want something to drink?"

She eyed a glass tumbler of iced liquid sitting atop a coaster on the coffee table. "What are you drinking?"

"Water."

"You surprise me," she said as she sat on the couch. The cushions shifted as he joined her.

"In what way?"

"I'm pretty good at guessing what people will order to eat and drink. Everything you've ordered has surprised me."

He lifted the glass, offering it to her. When she shook her head, he set it back down, then pulled his hand along the tumbler, sweeping up the condensation. Fascinated by his deliberate movements, she watched him shift toward her. She closed her eyes as he put his cold, wet hand against her throat and dragged his palm downward, his fingers following in its wake, cool and damp against her shower-warm skin. Her breath came in short, soft spurts as he slid his fingers under the edge of the robe. She arched forward; her breasts rose, seeking his touch. Instead, she felt him pull his hand away and draw a deep breath. She opened her eyes just as he brushed her hair with his fingertips.

"Do you mind if I loosen your braid?" he asked, his voice soft and gruff.

The pragmatic side of her wished he'd hurry up and get it over with. The tension was becoming unbearable. The long-celibate woman in her wished he'd take hours.

"I don't mind," she said, giving in to her heart's desire. She turned away from him, closing her eyes as she felt him pull off the band and work her hair out of its prison.

Patrick used his fingers as a comb as he released one strand after another of wavy white-blond hair into a flowing blanket down her back. "I've never known a woman with hair as long as yours," he said as he loosened the soft, fine hair, its strawberry fragrance filling the air around him, making his mouth water. "How long have you let your hair grow?"

Her head fell forward, and he wondered at her reaction. Was she pulling away or reacting to his question? Until that moment she had been luxuriating in his touch.

"I haven't cut it in six years."

"For any particular reason?"

"Yes."

He waited, but she added nothing. Her hair was free. The ends almost touched the sofa.

He sensed the mood had deteriorated and he wanted to rebuild it quickly, before it fell apart altogether. "Do you have a brush?" he asked, immediately regretting his words. He hadn't brushed a woman's hair since— Oh, God. Not since Priscilla. And she'd been so sick and her hair so lifeless, he'd wept as he brushed it. And *she* had comforted *him*.

Stop making comparisons. He hadn't thought about Priscilla this much in years. When he'd slept with a woman, he'd immersed himself in her, in her individuality, in her unique scent and feel. He'd never compared any woman to his wife. Not once. Until now.

Jasmine walked silently into the bathroom to get her brush from her purse. She glanced into the mirror before she left, seeing herself as he would, startled at the way she looked wearing the unfamiliar bathrobe, and with her hair loose. She edged closer. She'd been in such a daze when she'd gotten out of the shower, she hadn't reapplied any makeup, and she looked every one of her forty years. Catching a sigh of resignation in her throat, she padded back into the living room.

He sat exactly where she'd left him, his gaze on the fire, lost in thought. Was he missing his wife? Could she help him fill that void, just for a little while? Could he bring light into the black hole of her own losses, just for a little while? She held out the hairbrush as she came up to him.

He put his hand over hers and squeezed. "Losing your nerve?"

"No." She was surprised he even asked. "Why would you think so?"

"You were gone awhile."

She sat beside him, facing him, relinquishing the brush. "I was taking a hard look in the mirror."

"Why?" He indicated she should turn around, then he pulled the brush through her hair.

She closed her eyes and let herself enjoy the moment, stroke after stroke, the generosity of his gesture bringing her peace and unexpected sadness. Tears gathered behind her lids and she couldn't explain why. But there was more going on here than her wish for a baby, or his wish to ease loneliness. She was just too afraid to try to figure out what it all meant.

"Why, Jasmine? What did you see in the mirror that made you pause?"

The rhythm of his brushing lulled her. Excited her. Took her out of this world and into another, into a place far, far away from here. She stopped thinking about the past or the future. She focused only on the moment. "It doesn't matter," she said. "Just pretend you love me."

Patrick set the brush aside. He'd forgotten her request. He didn't know what he could do differently to make her feel loved.

He slid his hands around her and unfastened her belt, letting the robe fall open. Carefully, he grasped the loose sleeves and tugged, sliding them down her arms, until the fabric pooled at her hips. Grabbing her hair with his hands, he pushed it over her shoulders, then he flattened his palms against her back, letting them glide down her warm, pale skin and back up again. Across, down, up. Across again. Her flesh quivered. He heard her whisper his name. *Ba-boom*.

"You're so beautiful," he said, the words a deep whisper of need. He wanted to see her, all of her, and this time to touch her, hold her, make love to her. He put pressure on her arm, encouraging her to turn around. Leaving the robe behind, she climbed across his lap, straddling him. "You're so beautiful," he repeated as he pushed her hair back over her shoulders, exposing her glorious body. "Here." He cupped her breasts as he spoke, drawing a moan from her. "And here." *Ba-boom*. He ran his thumbs over the taut peaks as her head fell back and her hips shifted forward. He leaned toward her and caught a nipple in his mouth as a long moan came from her. His tongue learned her textures as his hands molded her.

"Harder? Lighter?" he asked as she moved abruptly, pushing herself against him tighter.

"D-doesn't matter. J-just don't stop."

He increased the pressure, then the suction, loving her response, the need she didn't attempt to hide. He shifted to the other breast and lavished his attention there until she began tugging at his T-shirt. She peeled it off him, following the fabric with her lips, her tongue tracing the midline of his chest from navel to throat. *Ba-boom*. Her thumbs brushed his nipples. Her breath came harsh and rapid against his skin.

Ba-boom. He needed her to stop for a minute, to let his heart settle down, but she moved against him, her breasts pressing into him, as she leaned closer and took his earlobe between her teeth. *Ba-boom*. He sucked in a deep breath and grabbed her shoulders to push her back.

"No," she moaned.

"Let's slow it down a little." He tried to hide his nervousness from her. In doing so, his words came out harsher than he'd wanted.

She crossed her arms protectively over her breasts. Her expression showed not only bewilderment but hurt. "Why?"

"So that we remember." He couldn't tell her the truth—that he was afraid. Afraid of the feelings he had for her, afraid of the memories she unwittingly made him dredge up. He plumped the pillows against the corner of the sofa and stretched out, drawing her to spoon with him, facing the fire. They lay there quietly for several minutes, although he never stopped stroking her. He couldn't get enough of her breasts, or the hard crests that had tasted so good, or the slightly rounded abdomen that would press against him when they finally came together.

"You have to take your jeans off," she said finally, breaking the silence. "It isn't fair. I'm naked and you're not." She turned to face him and slipped a hand between them.

Ba-boom.

The snap of his jeans sounded like a cannon blast; the zipper like machine gun fire. Her knuckles brushed his hardness. *Ba-boom.* She tugged at the fabric as he lifted himself, then she sat up to pull them all the way off, and his gaze followed the sway of her breasts as she moved. *Ba-boom.*

She tossed the jeans aside, then reached for his briefs. Ba-boom. Soon they joined his jeans in a heap on the floor. Their gazes met as she laid her hand over him. *Ba-boom. Ba-boom.*

"Don't." He caught her wrist and held tight. She smiled, a Mona Lisa expression that could mean anything, then she turned over and snuggled up to him, cradling him unerringly against her rear. *Ba-boom.*

He tried to think about business, the price per share of O'Halloran Shipping stock, the new contract he'd negotiated with Russia, the computer system he needed to replace. Nothing worked. His hands were full of her breasts, his head filled with her fragrance. He slid a hand down, over her abdomen, into the softness and heat of her womanhood. With feather-light touches he sought her, wanting to know what excited her the most, needing to know the feel of her, how hot, how wet she was. How ready.

Ready. Definitely ready. Was he?

"Night Flower," he said softly. "Shall we go to bed?"

She rolled over. "Kiss me first."

He hadn't kissed her, he realized. Except for the one last night and the brief kiss in the tub, they hadn't really kissed. He bent toward her, then stopped. *What are you afraid of?* The words reverberated loudly in his head. It's just a kiss. Just a kiss.

His lips touched hers, lightly teasing, then he discovered the joke was on him. Her mouth tasted of honey and need, hot, flowing, sweet, addictive. He slid his tongue into her mouth and met hers, pausing for a moment to savor before exploring further. He struggled for air as he changed the angle of the kiss; her moans vibrated up her throat and into her mouth, transferring to him. Again and again they kissed, their mouths opening wider, tongues moving, dueling, challenging.

Ba-boom. He dragged himself away, saw she was struggling to breathe also, then helped her up from the sofa to move into the bedroom. He left her standing by the bed as he stoked the fire. When he returned to her, he found her admiring him.

"You're beautiful, Patrick. All of you."

Her hair swirled around her, beckoning him closer. He tugged the comforter, blankets and sheet back in a flurry of cold air, leaving only the bottom sheet, a field of flowers suited to the English countryside. Night-blooming

Jasmine. What would she look like amid the colorful garden? He couldn't wait another minute to find out.

He guided her to stretch out on the bed, her pale body lustrous among the flowers. He moved over her. *Ba-boom.* Her legs opened to accommodate him. *Ba-boom.* He positioned himself at her entrance. *Ba-boom. Ba-boom.* She lifted her hips. *Ba-boom. Ba-boom. Ba-boom.*

He fought for breath as his pounding heart swelled in his throat. He pulled back.

"Patrick?"

The tension in her voice added to his own. What if he had a heart attack as he made love to her? *Ba-boom. Ba-boom.* What if he died in her arms? *Ba-boom. Ba-boom. Ba-boom.* He couldn't do it. He just couldn't do it.

"Patrick, what's wrong?"

His desire fled, but he recognized he still had an obligation to her. She hadn't made love in seven years. She needed him to pretend he loved . . .

He moved over her again and kissed her, a deep, unending kiss that he hoped would distract her from his obvious loss of arousal. The moment he took his mouth away, he slid down her, but she grabbed at him.

"What's wrong?" she asked, confusion in her voice.

"Nothing," he managed to say before he settled his mouth intimately against her and felt her lift up in surprise. *I can't give you what you need, so this will have to do,* he told her silently as he teased her with his tongue, tasted her, loved her.

Jasmine squirmed, trying to get him to move. She wanted—*needed*—him inside her. She pressed her palms against his head, curved her fingers into his hair.

"Relax. Enjoy it," he whispered, his breath stirring and warm, his tongue tempting her with slow strokes, drawing her loose of restraint, pulling her into a whirlwind of uncontrolled power. She forgot everything but sensation, the hot need that started where his mouth had settled, the teasing addition of his fingers that tormented, drawing long-denied hunger from deep inside her.

She called his name, hoarsely, longingly, with amazement and surprise at the strength of what he was giving her. She'd never felt anything like it, not this unending intensity, not this singular generosity.

She tried to clamp a hand over her mouth, but the sensations he drew from her again made her clutch the sheet with both hands and lift her hips, pressing herself even closer.

He shifted slightly, letting his tongue glide along her thigh, giving her a moment to calm. "No one can hear you," he said, accurately sensing her discomfort.

The moment she relaxed, he began his loving torture again. This time he didn't let up.

She stopped herself from screaming, but that was all. Tears flowed from her eyes, down her temples, into her hair, onto the bed. She writhed and lifted and rotated, this second time even stronger than the first. "Patrick, please. Please . . . You, too. Please."

He shifted off her as she felt the earth stop spinning. She wrapped a hand around his arm, trying to pull him to her, but he moved farther away, rolling to the side of the bed, where he sat, feet on the floor, head in his hands.

Bewildered, she sat up and slid close to him. His skin felt clammy beneath her hand. "What's wrong?" she asked.

After a full minute passed, he answered her. "I can't."

All the pleasure he had brought her dissipated at his words. She should have known, really. They were from two different worlds. She'd pushed him into this tonight, not really giving him any choice, before he'd had time to decide about her.

"I'll get dressed," she said, turning from him.

"Don't go. Please."

"But you don't want me."

His laugh was harsh. "I want you too much. That's the problem." He spoke to the ___ ___or. "But I *can't.* Do you understand what I'm saying? It isn't you. It's me. God, this is so embarrassing."

"But you were ready. I felt . . . I saw—"

"Well, it went away. I'm sorry. I tried to satisfy you anyway."

She pressed herself against his back, resting her chin on his shoulder. "You did, and then some. But are you sure, you know, about your condition?"

He shifted his shoulders, rubbing against her breasts and groaning. "I'm sure."

Jasmine considered what to say. Men were extraordinarily fragile when it came to sexual performance. If she said the wrong thing—

"That has never happened to me before, I swear it," he said vehemently. "I have never been . . . been—" he blew out a breath "—you know."

She hoped he could hear the smile in her voice as she teased him faintly. "Potency impaired?"

Six

A grin tugged at his mouth. The tension flowed out of his shoulders. "Is that the politically correct term these days?"

She kissed the sensitive spot just below his ear. "You loved your wife very, very much," she said.

Her words startled him. "I would have given my life for her."

"And you were faithful to her always."

"Of course I was."

She wrapped her arms around him and pressed her cheek to his. "So maybe you felt you were cheating on her. Not only is it understandable and forgivable, it's also admirable."

Chastising himself for the deceit, he grabbed at the excuse she so generously offered him, a lifeline to salvage his bruised ego. He hadn't ever wanted to please a woman so much. If he gave it a little time, maybe he still could. And himself. "Maybe you're right."

She nuzzled his neck. "I can go home, if you want. Or we could try again later. Tell me what you want."

Her breath feathered lightly over his ear; her breasts pillowed his back, offering comfort and promises of pleasure. "I want you, Night Flower."

"Then let's share each other's company. We have all night."

They settled comfortably and lay in silence for a long time, watching the fire die, stroking each other. Maybe he should confide in her, he thought. He recalled the stack of literature he'd been given when he left the hospital two weeks ago. Had there been something about letting the woman be on top, thus taking pressure off the man to do anything too strenuous? Yes, he could distinctly recall that now. He could tell Jasmine about his little problem and ask her to carry the burden.

But admitting it to her gave credibility to something he didn't want to believe, not fully. He'd denied his condition from the beginning because he'd felt too good. Too healthy. After four days in the hospital, he'd gone home to an empty house to recuperate, more tired from the hospital stay than the heart attack. But he'd passed his stress test with flying colors and been given permission to fly to San Francisco, provided he saw a local cardiologist, even though at first his doctor had said to wait another two weeks. Patrick would have come with or without permission; he finally convinced the doctor of that.

His life hadn't changed that much. The only indication now that he was dealing with a medical condition was the one aspirin he took daily and the tiny brown bottle of nitroglycerin tablets that he kept handy, just in case. And the new diet and exercise program. And a slew of fears he still hadn't put names to. And now, impotency.

That was all. Hardly anything, he thought with a twisted smile.

He'd checked in with the cardiologist his second day in San Francisco. Everything was going fine. There shouldn't be any reason for his inability to perform. The chances of a climax killing him were negligible. But he hadn't told anyone about his condition except his secretary, and he wanted it to stay that way. He'd even kept his daughter in the dark. So why would he share his fears with the beautiful woman in his arms?

He had to give it another try to see what happened.

Jasmine opened her eyes as Patrick's body changed from being a comfortable cushion to an unyielding bench. Guessing he thought it was time to try again but was afraid of what would happen, she pushed herself upright. "Roll onto your stomach."

He complied without protest. She rested her hands on his shoulders while she straddled him, then she kneaded his taut muscles, pleased when he groaned his pleasure.

"How long has it been since you've had a massage?" she asked.

"I've never had one like this."

She heard the smile in his voice. "Then we're even. I've never given one like this."

"You don't have to coddle me."

"It's not one-sided, Patrick. I find this extremely arousing to be able to touch you like this."

He shifted beneath her. "Your hair tickles."

"Is that bad?"

"I'm not sure."

She laughed as she turned her head side to side, letting her hair dance on his skin. She eased herself down his legs, kneading his buttocks as she shifted, admiring the sculpted beauty of his body.

"Falling asleep?" she asked after a few minutes.

"Oh, yeah. Right. Sure."

She smiled as she moved to kneel beside him. "Ready to roll over?"

He hesitated long enough for uncertainty to settle over her. She didn't want to rush him. And even if tonight was a failure, there might still be tomorrow. Finally, he turned over, and she saw that he was definitely not asleep, not any part of him.

She knew he was watching her, waiting for her. She ignored his aroused condition and instead picked up his right hand and pushed her thumbs into his palm with strong, circular motions. "Where did you get your calluses?" she asked, remembering the feel of his toughened hands against her skin, exciting and soothing. She watched him close his eyes and let himself relax as she didn't press him right away to begin making love.

"Loading freight."

"Uh-huh. And I'm actually a movie star researching the role of a waitress."

He grinned as he opened his eyes. "You don't believe me?"

"You're telling me you're a dock worker...who wears designer suits and attends exclusive clubs? I don't think so, Patrick."

"But it's the truth. I may spend more time in an office now than before, but I earned the calluses."

She leaned across him, intending to pick up his left hand.

"You're a beautiful woman, Night Flower." Patrick rose up and captured a nipple in his mouth. He surrounded her flesh with his hand, holding her still. "Climb over me," he said quietly, then helped her move. He lavished attention on her breasts as she leaned over him. *Ba-boom*. Their lower bodies skimmed, then settled, then glided. *Ba-boom*. *Ba-boom*. The more she moved, the more she moaned, the more his fear settled in. *Ba-boom*. *Ba-boom*. *Ba-boom*.

God. He couldn't do it. He couldn't. He was so damned afraid. His throat clamped shut with the pounding of his heart. A steady drumbeat reverberated in his ears. *Ba-boom. Ba-boom.* He knew the moment his desire faded. The exact, humiliating second.

To distract her, he sat up, shifting her to lie flat, then quickly caught her lips with his in a kiss that lasted a life-time and tasted like paradise, connecting them in an eter-nal bond. He learned her body with gentle hands, cherishing her, as his mouth continued to savor hers. Fi-nally he let his hand venture lower, creating a slow, steady arousal designed to bring her to fulfillment once more. *Ba-boom. Ba-boom. Ba-boom.*

"Patrick!" She raised her hips even as she struggled against him.

"Please," he pleaded with quiet desperation against her ear. "I need to do this for you. You have no idea how much I need—" He attacked her mouth with his, sharing his feelings with action rather than words. She must have sensed how important it was to him, because she finally let herself take what he offered, although her mouth went slack as her focus shifted to the newer, stronger sensa-tions bombarding her, and he pulled back a little to watch and remember.

Jasmine lay quietly in his embrace, her face pressed against his chest, his arms keeping her prisoner. She knew he thought he'd failed her, but it wasn't true. It was her failure, hers alone. She'd attempted to tamper with the sacred order that Maggie always touted, and not only had it backfired on her, it had included Patrick in the force of its retribution. Patrick, who still grieved for a well-loved wife. Patrick, who would make beautiful babies—but not hers.

Neither of them had spoken in the ten minutes since he'd gifted her yet again with pleasure while taking nothing for himself. Pretend he loved her? What a burden she'd placed on him, asking him for something that wasn't possible.

He tightened his hold as he spoke into her hair, his words soft and gruff. "I'm sorry."

She shook her head, afraid she would cry over the sound of his voice, so weary, so embarrassed.

"Stay with me, Night Flower."

She heard the anguish he tried to conceal. "I'll stay," she said, turning so that their bodies were spooned, snuggling closer to him as he pulled up the bed covers.

Minutes passed. He stroked her lightly, his callused hand offering comfort, his warm body making her feel as if she'd come home after years of wandering aimlessly. He would be so easy to care for, so easy to—

He murmured something as his arm became deadweight around her waist.

I love you? Was that what he said? Or was it her imagination?

Jasmine pressed a hand to her mouth, preventing any sound from escaping. Had he just been playing the role she'd assigned him—or were the words the last thing he'd said to his wife each night? After all these years, she had finally given herself to a man—and he didn't want her. She'd found his fatal flaw.

The irony should have made her laugh. Instead tears spilled in scalding streaks down her face and into the pillow. She hadn't done anything to deserve having her children stolen from her. She'd been a good mother, a loving mother. And she didn't deserve to be alone for the rest of her life.

And Patrick hadn't deserved her dishonesty, even though much of the time she'd forgotten her real reasons for being with him tonight.

It was time to cut her losses. She hadn't met anyone remotely acceptable in the six months before Patrick's arrival on the scene, and his inability to perform seemed to be merely the ending punctuation on her quest to be a mother again.

The journey had ended. Her path was set. Alone.

After a while she eased out of bed and looked at him, her heart aching a little. Yes, he would be so easy to love.

She backed out of the room, dressed in her still-damp clothes and made a silent escape from the cottage, the man and her dreams.

She didn't even let me take her home. Patrick let the drape fall, then leaned his forehead against the cool wall. The rain had begun in earnest again, and he didn't know when she'd left. Had she gotten drenched? Had she made it home safely?

Ah, Night Flower. You chose the wrong man to end your drought with.

He glanced at the mantel clock: 2:10. He couldn't have slept more than half an hour. He'd awakened a few minutes ago and reached for her, finding only a damp pillow. Tears? he wondered. Guilt piled upon guilt.

Shivering, he picked up the bathrobe that lay pooled on the floor beside the sofa and slid into it. She hadn't worn it long enough to leave her scent on the fabric. Maybe that wasn't so bad. The pillow had carried a trace of strawberry when he'd pressed his face into it. That had been hard enough to handle.

Wishing for a healthy dose of Scotch, he busied himself by putting away the chairs he'd arranged to hang up her wet clothes. His still lay over a chair in the bedroom, and he scooped them up to drape over the shower rod.

He wandered back to the living room, stoked the fire and sank onto the couch, staring at the floor. On the dark carpet at his feet lay a long blond hair, glistening in the firelight. With utmost care, he picked it up to finger the length over and over, then wound it around his wrist and stared at the bracelet it made, stark white against his tanned skin.

Priscilla had been brunette, and taller, and more finely boned. She'd been a scrapper from the first day he'd met her, someone who loved to debate, as well as to play practical jokes. And she'd had the most infectious laugh, rich and appreciative and full of the devil.

He'd clung to her memory for so long, so very long.

And he was so tired of being alone.

Jasmine was . . . soothing and gentle and forgiving. And he'd hurt her with his dishonesty.

Could he somehow make it up to her? Would she let him try? Would she believe anything he said now?

He'd built his business by taking risks. He could rebuild his life the same way.

"You're doing *what?*"

Maggie's words echoed in the staff locker room. Jasmine had assumed a military stance to make her announcement. She avoided looking at her sister by bending to retie a perfectly tied shoelace. "I am taking two weeks' vacation, starting now. I called Gloria. She said she'd be glad to fill in."

"Why?"

"She could really use the money—"

"Jazz! Why are you taking vacation? You never take vacation. You're never even sick. What's going on?"

Jasmine straightened slowly. "I need some time away."

"What about your other job?"

She didn't need to avoid her day job. Patrick didn't know about it. "I'll be there."

"You're taking a vacation only from the club?"

"That's right."

Maggie crossed her arms over her chest. "So what happened between you and hubba-hubba?"

"Noth—"

"Liar."

"Okay." The word came out harsh and impatient. She gentled her tone. "Okay. *Something.* But I don't want to talk about it."

"Did he hurt you, Jazz?" Her voice, soft and caring, settled over Jasmine like a down comforter.

"No. He's surprisingly gentle." *And vulnerable.* "It's just . . . complicated."

"Honey, that man is worth a complication or two."

"And therein lies the problem."

"Listen, Jazz, your life is about as adventurous as a windshield wiper on a rainy day. To work, to home, to work, to home. Back and forth, back and forth. What's wrong with a little diversion? He's on vacation, so you know it has to end. It wouldn't have time to develop into another situation like with Deacon."

No, this would be much worse. This is a man capable of loving until death. This is a man of integrity. Jasmine turned her back on her sister. *I love you.* The words she'd chosen to believe he'd uttered made a bed in her heart, flounced around a little, seeking the right spot, then settled. He'd said them as part of the role he'd been playing for her, or maybe just out of habit. He couldn't have known how much she'd needed to hear them, or how the peace she'd found in his arms terrified her as much as it soothed her. "Nothing's going to happen between us," she said to Maggie, who had just finished knotting her tie and was dressed for work. "It's better to stop it now."

"I still don't think it's worth taking a vacation over," Maggie muttered. "If he comes in, you deal with it. Maybe he won't even be back, and then what have you done? Taken vacation for nothing."

"You're just upset because your wedding dress fund will suffer for a while."

"I am not!"

Jasmine smiled, breaking the tension. "Tell J.D. I won't need him to walk home with me, okay? He'll probably be glad to be relieved of the responsibility. He's been spending a lot of time with—what's her name, anyway?"

"Adrianna." Maggie turned the name into a sneer. "Gold digger."

"How can she be a gold digger when he doesn't have any money?"

Maggie tossed her head. "He's not going to be a maître d' forever. Anyone can see that. *Adrianna* sniffed him out for his potential."

"Why, Magnolia Walters, you sound positively jealous." Jasmine watched her sister's cheeks flush pink, stark contrast to her alabaster skin.

"I'm possessive, I'll grant you that. He's been like a brother to both of us. You have to admit, you're interested in how his life turns out. More interested than the average, considering his history. That doesn't make me jealous. He's too macho, anyway."

"He's gentle when it matters."

Maggie closed her locker a little too forcefully. "I don't have time to date. Between work and college—"

"Did I mention dating?" Jasmine asked innocently. "Let me think. No, I'm sure I didn't. Although now that you mention it—"

Maggie smiled sweetly. "It's getting late, Jazz. Some of us have to work."

"Later than you think, darling sister. Not even a year until your thirtieth birthday. You have to date to find a man. And J.D. is so...convenient."

"Night-night, honey. Sunday supper, my place, as usual?" Maggie strolled past, hips swaying.

"Sure." As soon as Maggie reached the door, Jasmine added, "Invite J.D., too."

Maggie laughed but kept going. Jasmine's grin faded slowly as she stood in the middle of the locker room feeling more alone than she had for a long time. Tempted to stay and secretly learn whether Patrick returned to the club, she instead made a noiseless exit from the building and walked home.

"She's not here."

Patrick interpreted the look on J.D.'s face to mean more than the words he'd just uttered quietly. "Where is she?"

"Vacation."

Patrick winced. "Unplanned, I take it."

"Yes, sir." He waited a beat. "Perhaps you would like something stronger than club soda tonight?"

Yeah, like maybe a whole bottle of Scotch. Pain pierced him, a stinging sensation he chose to believe came from Nurse Crackwhip's voodoo doll, not the absence of one blond American beauty with the compact body, mysterious name and heart full of disillusion about the male gender.

"When will she be back?" he asked the younger man who stood silently waiting, sympathy reflected in his dark brown eyes.

"Two weeks, she says."

Long enough for me to be gone. "Thank you for telling me."

"Will you be staying for dinner, sir?"

He was supposed to have an appetite? He rubbed his forehead. Well, he needed to eat somewhere. If not here, then he would undoubtedly choose some fast-food place. Crackwhip shouldn't have too many opportunities in one night. "Could I order something to go?"

"Of course. I will send Magnolia over."

"Do you think that's a good idea?"

J.D. grinned. "Maybe. Maybe not. Her fuse was lit when she told me earlier."

"Volatile, huh?"

"Possessive. Like a tigress." J.D. leaned closer. "Watch your back."

"Thanks." Patrick's gaze shifted to Maggie as she made her way to his table. He watched J.D. intercept her and say something. She shook her head. He said something else. She shrugged. He bent closer and whispered in her ear. She swayed toward him, then straightened, pushing back her shoulders.

This was going to be the toughest negotiation he'd ever entered into, Patrick decided.

"How could you mess things up so fast?" she asked without preamble.

"It's a talent."

She laughed, even though he could tell she didn't want to.

"Did she tell you what happened?" he asked.

"She's not layin' any blame at your feet, if that's what you're askin', honey."

Ah, the drawl had thickened—which meant either she had relaxed or she was about to pounce.

"Any suggestions, Miss Magnolia?"

"The halibut is fresh."

Patrick grinned. No help from this corner.

"What do you intend to do about it?" she asked.

"Try again."

"You have the time to wait her out?"

"I can make the time."

"Patience?"

"Never been known for it. But there's a first time for everything." *And when you've been reborn, you get to start over and learn new things.*

Seven

Jasmine was not in a good mood. The uncertainties that faced her were bad enough. Had Patrick left town? If he hadn't, would he be at the club tonight upon her return? But the certainty was even worse—she'd started her period this morning, incontrovertible evidence of a missed opportunity.

She slammed her locker door. Maggie hadn't been any help, either, not telling her whether Patrick was still around. For two weeks she'd worked at not being grouchy with the customers at the diner where she spent her afternoons. Instead she'd focused her excess energy on her small apartment, first scraping and sanding woodwork during the late afternoon and evening, then painting until two or three o'clock in the morning.

Next she'd relined her shelves and reorganized every drawer. All fourteen tenants of the apartment complex were happy recipients of her black mood when it led to a baking binge that lasted several days and resulted in dozens of cookies, four pies, three cakes and two varieties of bread that she divvied up, leaving herself the lion's share.

Five pastry-rich pounds had made themselves at home on her hips before she'd slowed down and taken a good look at what she was doing. Her life had been just fine—considering—before Patrick O'Halloran had arrived on the scene. It would be just fine again.

"You're early."

Jasmine turned. Maggie stood slouched against the doorjamb, as if she'd been there forever.

"I was antsy," Jasmine said, starting to walk past her. "Figured I'd come in and get the salt and peppers done."

"He hasn't been here for days. Almost a week."

Was that relief that flooded her? Jasmine wondered. Something strong and reactionary, anyway. "Good."

"Uh-huh."

Jasmine ignored the sarcastic retort and headed for the kitchen. She *was* glad. Grateful. Pleased. *Thrilled.* She didn't ever want to see him again, be tempted by him again. She wasn't some teenager who yearned for someone to love her to the exclusion of all else. She was mature, realistic, and sensible. She'd learned that if something seemed too good to be true, it probably was. He had seemed perfect for her needs.

And now her needs had changed. During the past two weeks she had given up the idea of having a baby. It had been a lovely fantasy, something that had allowed her to dream once again, something to give her hope. Now she could go back to her old life, which was safe and predictable and free of men with their impossible demands and needs. Free of men who took what they wanted, then disappeared, sometimes with your most precious possessions.

Men. The good ones got married and stayed married. They came home at night, kissed their wives, and tossed their children in the air. They offered a shoulder to lean on and a listening heart. They were happy with a woman who loved them and children who begged for a game of horsey, not a showpiece on their arm and proper angels who never spilled milk or scraped knees.

There were good men out there, somewhere. In the arms of good women. Women like her were temporary solutions to pressing problems, usually sexual, but sometimes to aid in someone's rebellion, like Deacon, who'd wanted to defy his parents and their money and expectations. In the end, he'd used her, as so many men had used her mother. Just as Jasmine had contemplated using a man to get what she'd wanted.

She wouldn't use or be used again.

The sound of a quarter hitting the bottom of an empty ceramic jar reverberated in the kitchen. Back to life as usual.

He'd never seen anything so beautiful. Patrick slid into the booth J.D. pointed out and watched Jasmine unobtrusively pick up empty dinner plates, not interrupting the conversation of the two couples seated at a table twenty feet away. She happened to glance his direction. Even from that distance, he saw her cheeks flush and her body stiffen.

As reactions went, it was minimal... and could mean anything—anger, pleasure. No, not pleasure. She had just spent two weeks avoiding him. Embarrassment, maybe? Hell, she didn't have anything to be embarrassed about. *He* did. He'd failed her. It had taken every bit of courage he had to confide his disgrace to his cardiologist, who had cautioned patience and insisted that there was no physical reason for his being... potency impaired.

It was a challenge, all right. One of the biggest of his life. And he would rise to the occasion, he thought, smiling. He just had to convince Jasmine to give him another chance.

She marched to his table. He followed her movements appreciatively.

"I'm not waiting on you," she announced.

He recognized bravado when he saw it—and embarrassment. "It's nice to see you, too."

"I'll send Maggie over to take your order."

"How was your vacation?"

She frowned. "I don't want to talk to you, either."

"I guess it wasn't restful. You're pretty keyed up for having just had two weeks off."

"Stop it, Patrick."

"Stop what?"

"Making conversation, as if nothing happened between us."

He slid his jacket off and passed it to her. "Would you mind hanging this up?"

She accepted the garment automatically, folded it over her arm, stroked the fabric without conscious thought. He refused to smile.

"Why are you still here?" she asked.

"I'm going to have dinner."

"In San Francisco," she clarified, her eyes narrowing.

"Why do you think?"

"Your daughter is still out of town?"

"Actually, she's been and gone again. I spent the last week with her."

"So that's why you weren't…" Her words faded as she realized what she was admitting.

"Keeping tabs on me, Jasmine?"

She shrugged. "Maggie mentioned it. I didn't ask," she added with a little too much force.

"Of course not."

"I didn't."

"I believe you. So, you're pretty ticked off, huh?"

"I have to get to work. I'll send Maggie."

He laid his hand on hers, bringing her aware of her action as she continued to stroke his jacket. "I was afraid you hadn't gotten home safely. I didn't even know your last name. I can't believe I didn't know that before we— I had no way of finding out if you were okay."

"Safe and sound, as you can see." She walked away from him unhurriedly, stopping to speak to Maggie, who looked in Patrick's direction and nodded.

He conceded round one to her.

In the privacy of the coat closet, Jasmine gave in to overwhelming need and slipped Patrick's jacket on. Just for a few seconds. Well . . . maybe for a minute. Just a few seconds more. She needed a hug, and this would have to do. It was supposed to warm her, but she started shaking instead, violently, uncontrollably. She trembled as she pulled off the jacket and hung it up. Damn him. Damn him for making her feel things again. Damn him for being a confident man who hadn't the slightest inkling what he was doing to her. Damn him for the take-a-chance looks he gave her and the promises in his eyes. He was just a man. One of those good men who married good women, women of their own station. Women who hadn't failed so miserably that they couldn't risk failing again.

Damn him for making her wish she could be different.

He waited in the lobby until midnight, when the doors were about to be locked. Then he waited outside. She never came. She'd left through another exit.

He shoved his hands into his pockets and walked back to his hotel room. Round two—Jasmine.

"Mr. O'Halloran didn't come back tonight," J.D. said as he and Jasmine walked home the following evening.

"No."

"How do you feel about that?"

"Relieved."

A scruffy-looking man approached them. J.D. fired him a *back-off* glare.

"Maybe he was only looking for a handout," she said, watching the man continue down the street.

"At midnight? Not likely. Haven't I taught you better in all these months? Even the panhandlers—"

"I know. I *know*. 'You give them money, they won't rise above it.' The world according to J. D. Duran."

"It's true."

"But the nights are lonely and the streets cold. I have enough to share a little."

"You are not so generous with Mr. O'Halloran."

"What could I give him that he doesn't have or couldn't get easily enough somewhere else?"

"It makes me sad you think so little of yourself, Jasmine."

She'd always loved the way he said her name, with the slightest accent tying him to his heritage. He'd worked hard at getting rid of it. "Flatterer," she said with a grin. "Maggie tells me things are serious with you and this Adrianna."

White teeth flashed in response. "Ah, yes. The lovely Adrianna. So willing, so energetic."

"Are you going to marry her?"

"Adrianna is not the kind of woman a man marries."

"Why not?"

"She has given herself too many times to too many men. She is a pleasant companion, but her morals are lacking."

Jasmine cocked her head at him. "Not lacking enough, apparently, for you not to enjoy them."

He shrugged. "Double standards. I'm aware of the concept. Still, I will marry a woman pure of heart."

"And body?"

"Not necessarily. But she can't be free with herself. Do you understand?"

"A woman like, say, Maggie," she said pointedly.

He closed his eyes briefly and smiled. "Magnolia." He gave her name an interesting inflection, as well. "Magnolia is fire and smoke."

"What am I?"

"Moonlight and cool water."

She smiled. "If you were just a few years older, J. D. Duran..." she said, teasing him.

"You know it isn't years that separate us, Jasmine, but fire."

They stopped at the bottom steps of her apartment house. "Yes, I know. And I like knowing you are just my friend. We don't have a complicated relationship."

"Jasmine."

They turned in unison to see Patrick walk out of the darkness toward them.

"We need to talk," he said.

She looked helplessly at J.D.

"You're safe with him," he said, nodding at them, then striding away without looking back.

"We've said everything, Patrick." Jasmine leaned against a railing and pulled her coat more tightly to her.

He crowded her space, but she didn't take a step up. "You don't give second chances, I guess. Funny, I had you figured for someone who didn't expect everyone to be perfect. People fail, Jasmine. I failed. I'm sorry about that. I'd like a second chance."

"I can't, Patrick. I just can't. For more reasons than I can tell you. Please, don't pressure me."

"I know I didn't give you what you needed. I can't apologize enough for that."

"Don't reduce this to sex. I'm forty, not twenty. I know that sex isn't perfect all the time. Or predictable. Or even necessary. I know it was embarrassing for you. But that's not what this is about."

"I'm not talking only about sex, either. I enjoy your company. You're easy to be with."

I want to be someone's fire, she thought desperately, fighting tears that threatened at the realization. She wanted to be *his* fire. She wanted to be courted, wooed, fawned over. She wanted all the silly things she'd declared forever didn't matter, instead scoffing about how they were games, not real life. Not even preparation for real life. And yet she wanted it. To be romanced. To be treasured. To be loved. By this man.

She wanted to make love with him for the pure pleasure of it. She wanted the freedom to explore him, to challenge him to a duel of bodies, a duel to the little death, simultaneous and mutually satisfying, as perspiration beaded on their skin and the outside world ceased to exist.

With this man. This impossible man.

"Night Flower," he said softly, moving closer.

Impossible. "Don't you have a job to get back to? A life?"

Patrick stared at her, trying to recall his job, his life. His job had consumed him for almost thirty years. His life? He'd lived on the edge for a long time, taking huge, potentially business-ending risks to build his company. He'd worked twelve, fourteen, sixteen hours a day for as long as he could remember. He'd thrived on adrenaline. He'd raised a daughter he had just now begun communicating honestly with after years and years of trying to be both mother and father—and failing. He was damned lucky she'd turned out as well as she had, and that she'd forgiven him his many mistakes.

He'd had a heart attack.

Did he want to go back to his job? Maybe. To his life? No. Absolutely, unequivocally, no.

He was aware of how still Jasmine was, how she was waiting for him to back away. "Could we go to your apartment and talk?" he asked.

"This has to end. You have to stop seeking me out."

"I don't think I can."

"Go home, Patrick. Please."

Hearing the quiet desperation in her voice, he backed away. One step. Two. She didn't move, didn't turn from him. Her eyes begged him to come back even as she crossed her arms as if to hold him at bay.

He couldn't leave it like this. He took one long stride, pulled her into his arms and kissed her, tasting honey and heat. Soft little sounds came from within her as she clung to him, returning his kiss with fervent need. When he would have gentled the kiss, she demanded harshness. When he wanted to tame the moment into a treasured memory, she forced recklessness. Struggling for air, she pulled her mouth from his and burrowed her head against his shoulder, and he held her, cherished her, for an eternal minute.

"This doesn't change anything," she said, rubbing her cheek against his chest. "Your late wife stands between us. You're obviously not ready for a relationship yet. But more importantly—and something that won't change with time—we're from two different worlds."

He decided it was probably safer not to tell her the truth about Priscilla yet. But the other issue he could clarify. "I've worked hard all my life, Jasmine. My father died when I was twenty-four. He left me a legacy of a nearly bankrupt shipping company and twenty employees who depended on me to continue to provide them jobs. I worked night and day to do that. I took a company that should have been plowed under and turned it into a success. *I* did it. I loaded and unloaded freight. I wore out shoes going from company to company, drumming up business. I stayed in fleabag hotels overseas while I wore my one good suit and negotiated contracts with European markets. I got into fights because of where I stayed and because I got mad over the injustices in my life.

"You think I belong to some upper-crust Boston society? I circle the perimeter because of what my business is now. I'm invited in at times because I am a success, so they can't ignore me. But in the end I'm just a cubic zircona in a crown of diamonds. And I keep waiting to be exposed for the fraud I am."

The last thing Jasmine wanted was for Patrick to become more real, more of a person, with faults and failings and weaknesses. Deacon, too, had been an imperfect man, easy to love at first. But he'd discovered he missed living among the rich and famous, and she wasn't a woman who fit in with that crowd. She'd worked since she was twelve. Idleness wasn't part of her makeup. In the end she'd been too "plebeian," as Deacon had called her, too common. Patrick's world wouldn't change for her. And she couldn't change for it.

She stepped back. "I hope you find someone wonderful, Patrick. You deserve it."

"I thought I had," he said quietly. Then he turned and walked away.

She didn't watch him go. Instead she jogged the stairs to her third-floor apartment so that all she had to think about for a while was refilling her lungs.

Eight

Patrick yielded round three to Jasmine by the narrowest of margins. Time to change tactics, he decided as he let himself into Rye and Paige's house the next morning. He headed straight for their office to retrieve some requested information from their file cabinet to fax to them in the Cayman Islands, where they were hot on the trail of another embezzler.

That Paige had been surprised he was still in San Francisco had been obvious during their early-morning phone call.

"Why are you still there, Dad?" she had asked. "And this time tell me the truth."

"Enjoying my freedom, kid," he'd answered.

"I thought you were going home after we left. We had a great week together, but you've been away from the company for more than two weeks. This is totally unlike you."

"People change. I told you when I first settled the merger that I wanted to be out in the field again, not tied to a desk. I've just gone cold turkey, that's all."

"You're arranging West Coast business for the company?"

He'd heard the skepticism in her voice. "I'm definitely looking at West Coast possibilities."

Silence. Then, "Have you met a woman?"

Patrick had grinned at her you'd-better-answer-this-question-and-I-mean-right-now tone of voice. "I don't kiss and tell." She'd muffled the telephone and said something to Rye, who'd immediately gotten on the line.

"Patrick?"

Ah. Rye, the soother. He'd had his I'll-handle-this voice on. "Rye."

"What's going on?"

"Nothing that you'd be interested in."

"*Have* you met a woman?"

"Since I've been here? Sure. Dozens. Why?" He'd grinned harder. They'd pestered him all last week about how he'd spent his time, and he hadn't revealed anything. Why would he now?

"Who is she?"

Patrick had stayed silent. Rye had taken the hint. He'd asked Patrick to pull some information from a file in his office and fax it to him. That had been two hours ago. Since then he'd had breakfast, taken a walk and then driven to Rye and Paige's house, all the while plotting his next move with Jasmine.

He retrieved the key to the file cabinet from the wall safe, popped the lock, then opened the drawer labeled H-L.

The doorbell chimed and he turned, wondering whether he should answer it. When it rang again, he moved silently into the living room and peered into the peephole. He yanked the door open.

"Patrick!"

Jasmine took a surprised step back. He grabbed her just before she stumbled down the stoop.

"Are you all right?" he asked.

"What are you doing here?"

"This is my daughter's home."

"Paige? Paige is your daughter? Rye is your son-in-law?"

"That's right. Please. Come in." He tugged lightly on her arm.

"I don't think—"

"I won't bite."

Jasmine got lost in his smile. Blindly, she followed until they stood in the living room, the front door shut behind them. Her mind whirled. Paige's father. What if she *had* gotten pregnant? By Paige's *father?* The thought made her weak. Keeping his child a secret would have been impossible. She'd been lucky he couldn't make love to her. Just plain lucky. Someone had actually been looking out for her.

"So, you know my daughter."

"Yes. No. That is, we've met once. I've known Rye for years." She watched Patrick's face cloud with questions. "Not intimately. Would you get him, please? I really need to talk to him."

"He and Paige are out of town. They were home last week, then left again."

She looked at the floor, hiding her disappointment. "How long will they be gone?"

"It's hard to tell. A week maybe. Jasmine?"

"What?"

"Are you in some kind of trouble?" he asked. "Can I help you with anything?"

She lifted her head. "I'm fine. I was surprised to see you here, that's all. If you could find me a piece of paper, I'll just leave him a note."

"I have his phone number. You could call him."

His curiosity was evident. She liked that he didn't pressure her for answers.

"That's all right. It isn't urgent." *Yet.* "A note will do."

"Let's go to his office."

She sat at the desk to pen a quick note, then hunted for an envelope. Patrick rummaged through the file drawer, pulled out a folder and set it on the desk across from her. He thumbed through the papers, finally pulling one out to read thoroughly as she sealed the envelope shut and wrote Rye's name on the front.

"Why are you going through Rye's files?" she asked.

"This is the one they want," he said to himself as he stood and moved to the other side of the room. "Because they need some information and the person who usually helps wasn't available. I was. Do you know how to work this?"

"What is it?"

"A fax machine."

"Nope. You mean you don't?"

"My secretary takes care of that sort of thing."

"Then I guess you need to ask your secretary. Goodbye, Patrick."

He continued to study the machine. She slowed her steps, waiting for him to acknowledge her leaving.

"You could fax your note to him," he said, not looking at her. "I'm sending him this page now. Or whenever I get it figured out."

"That's okay. It can wait until he gets back. Goodbye."

"'Bye."

Jasmine frowned. "Take care of yourself," she said.

"You, too." He punched a button. A dial tone sounded from the speaker.

"Um, thanks. I will." She took one more step, then stopped as he punched in a lot of numbers. He jammed the piece of paper in the machine. A phone rang, then a long beep pierced the air. The paper just sat there.

"Damn. Didn't take it." Patrick picked up the receiver to break the connection. He was very aware of Jasmine, poised to flee. He hadn't planned this strategy—ignoring her—but it seemed to be working just fine. She wanted his attention because he wasn't giving her any. He wondered how long he could fake incompetency. "Maybe the paper has to be in before I dial."

He knew she hadn't left, even though she said nothing. He positioned the paper then started to dial the number.

"Hit the redial," she said.

He looked at her as if surprised she was still there. "Huh?"

She moved closer. "Even I know that much. You don't have to dial all the numbers again. Just push redial."

"Oh. Thanks." He felt her come up beside him. He smelled strawberries and sunshine. It took everything he had not to take her in his arms and hold on for dear life. He punched redial.

They listened to a repetition of the first attempt. Dial tone, beeps, ring, long beep. Nothing. The paper didn't budge.

She shouldered her way closer. "What's that button for?" she asked, pointing to one marked Start Copy. "Maybe if you hit that button."

Barely an inch separated their bodies. Patrick pushed the Start Copy button. The machine pulled the paper in as he leaned forward to smell her hair.

"Bingo!" Happy at her success, she jerked her head up to look at him—and collided with his chin. "Patrick! Oh, my gosh. I'm so sorry. Are you hurt?"

He doubled over and cradled his jaw with his hand. She crouched to his level.

"Can you talk?" she asked. "Can you move your jaw?"

"How's your head?" he mumbled, shifting his jaw back and forth and wincing.

"It hurts. Are you okay?"

"I'm okay." He worked his jaw a few seconds longer. "You could kiss it and make it better."

Their eyes met. She straightened at the same time he did. Gently, she pressed her lips to his chin. He ducked his head and caught her mouth with his.

"Jasmine," he whispered between kisses. "Jasmine."

Her name sounded lovely, she thought as she returned the pressure and enjoyed the taste of him. After long, barren years, she'd finally begun dreaming again, but the dream hadn't come close to reality. He was all male— power and hunger and intrigue, gentleness and need and desire.

He curved a hand over her rear and pulled her closer. She rubbed her breasts against his chest, turning slightly in invitation. No one could accuse him of being slow. He immediately brought a hand up to cup her breast and thumb a nipple, hard with need.

"Let's go to the sofa," he said, quietly, roughly, as he yanked her blouse from her waistband.

"I can't," she groaned.

"It'll be better this time."

She clamped her hands on his arms, holding him still. She hadn't had to share such intimate information with anyone in years. "I *can't*. Do you understand? I'm... indisposed."

Patrick assimilated the words. His heart settled down now that the pressure was off. He'd hoped if they didn't plan things, everything would work the way it should. Now he didn't have to worry about anything at all.

He grabbed her hand and tugged her toward the couch.

"Patrick—"

"Want to pretend we're teenagers? Remember climbing in the back seat of a car and necking? We can do that, okay?"

"Okay."

He heard surprise in her voice, and maybe a little disbelief. She had no idea how relieved he was, therefore how true to his word he could be. He helped her straddle his lap, letting her take the lead and set the pace for a while. She seemed to need a lot of kissing, so he gave her that— no great hardship on his part. When he lifted his hands to the buttons on her blouse, she pushed back a little, giving him better access. As he unfastened the last button, she laid her hands over his. He saw her cheeks flush rosily.

"What's wrong?" he asked.

"I—I didn't expect this today. Didn't dress for this. I'm afraid I didn't wear anything too...exciting."

He pushed her blouse aside, revealing the plain nude-colored bra beneath. She watched him smile, then their gazes met.

"It turns me on. *You* turn me on, Night Flower."

The tension melted away. She helped him take off her blouse, watched him lay it carefully aside. He spent a long time teasing the edges of the bra before he finally unfastened the hooks in back and pulled the garment down and off.

"You're even more beautiful in daylight," he said, his eyes focused on the flesh that quivered and swelled, begging his touch. He glanced at the window to the left of them.

"Scoot off," he said. She shifted as he slid out from under her, went to the window and opened the shutters, letting the sun pour in. Then he resituated them, propping his back against the arm of the sofa so that she faced the sun, still straddling him, her torso in a spotlight of sunshine.

"Nice," he said. "Very, very nice." His hands stayed busy a long time, before he finally took a pebbled nipple in his mouth and savored her. She moaned with pleasure as he circled the hard peak with his tongue, his teeth scraping gently before he pulled her flesh deep into his mouth and drew sustenance from her femininity.

Jasmine arched her back, pushing herself farther into his mouth. He slid down to lie flat so that she leaned over him and he drew one nipple then the other into his mouth.

"Incredible breasts," he said, his voice husky and full of need.

"Is that your favorite?" she asked as he bit lightly.

"Sometimes." He pulled her down and kissed her, open-mouthed and hungrily. "Sometimes it's your mouth." He dragged his lips along her jaw to capture her earlobe. "Sometimes this." He slid both hands over her rear, his fingers meeting in the middle, where they curved and held and pulled slightly until she gasped. "And sometimes this."

He pushed her up so that he could sit, and she yanked the buttons on his shirt free and shoved it off him. They glided together, perspiration creating a slick surface. They watched as their flesh touched, created electricity, burned.

Patrick rolled her beneath him, nudged her legs apart and settled himself, the placket of his jeans pressing into the juncture of her legs, the light fabric of her pants hardly a barrier at all. He started the rhythm even as she started to protest. He needed this—this one step at a time of making love. One beautiful step at a time. Soon, some-time soon, he'd be able to take her to the heavens and he could go with her. Soon. But for now—

"Wrap your legs around me," he ordered, low and quiet. "Night Flower, you feel so good. Don't push it. Just let it happen. Let me stay like this with you for a while." He went still as he sensed she was ready to peak, and she groaned, loud and long. "Shh. Shh. Relax. Let yourself settle down for a minute."

"Patrick—"

The word was a plea, a demand. He pressed forward again and rotated. Instantly her hips arched up to meet him. When her body grew taut, he pulled away again. She tried to follow, then fell back against the sofa, panting, begging him, pulling him toward her. He kissed her instead. Her mouth was on fire.

"You burn me alive," he said against her ear.

"I do? *I* do?" she asked, stilling a moment.

"You're like flames beneath me, burning me up." He moved back to look at her face, and he didn't understand what he saw in her eyes—gratitude, maybe, then tears. Then her eyes closed, her body arched, her mouth fell open, and she groaned her satisfaction as he moved in fierce rhythm against her, almost taking the journey with her before his heart began to pound relentlessly in his ears and chest. Suddenly afraid, he held his breath, waiting for what would happen. But everything quieted down as she slowed her movements beneath him, then relaxed into the cushions.

He pressed his cheek to hers, felt the dampness of perspiration and tears. "Why are you crying?" he asked, not lifting his head, giving her privacy.

Jasmine tightened her arms around him. *Because I'm your fire.* "I have to get up," she said, pushing at him, needing to leave the security and safety of his embrace before she wallowed in it. She felt his eyes on her as she scooped up her bra.

"Don't turn your back," he said, rising up on an elbow to watch.

She glanced at him.

"Don't hide. I've already seen and admired all of you."

She leaned forward, letting her breasts fill the cups of her bra, at the same time noting that he was still aroused.

"I could do something about that—" she gestured with a hitch of her head "—if you'd like."

She watched him pass a hand over the bulging placket of his jeans. She wanted to please him, as he had pleased her. She didn't want to just take from him all the time.

"C'mere," he said, holding out a hand.

When she got close, he turned her around to sit in front of him, then he hooked her bra and helped her slip into her shirt.

He reached around to fasten her buttons, starting with the bottom and working slowly upward. Her gaze focused on the dark wood file cabinet. He worked the second button. She glanced at the label on the open file drawer. H-L. He eased the third button in. She realized that her folder would be in that drawer. The fourth button. Did he still not know her last name? The fifth.

She jumped up, tucking in her shirt as she moved across the room. Scooping the paper from the fax machine, she returned it to the open file folder. "I'll put this away, then we can leave together, okay?"

Patrick picked up his shirt. "Okay," he said slowly, standing. "Would you like a ride somewhere?"

"You have a car?"

"I'm borrowing Paige's convertible."

"Oh. Well, I need to get home. I'm expecting a call."

"All right." He couldn't figure out her quick change of mood. She pushed the file into the drawer, slammed it shut and shoved in the lock. He'd almost declared round four his, then she'd started acting strangely. Now what? he wondered. What wall did he have to scale this time?

He returned the key to the safe and made sure everything else was in order. His gaze flickered across the envelope she'd addressed to Rye. Curiosity melded with jealousy—she trusted Rye but not him.

"Let's go," she said, tugging on his hand, her smile overly bright.

There was a mystery here, one she didn't want to clue him in on. One he intended to solve.

Nine

—

She didn't tell him not to try to see her again. *She* gave *him* a goodbye kiss. She smiled at him and waved as he pulled away from the curb.

Something wasn't right.

Patrick followed the feeling back to his daughter's house and let himself in. He strode into the office and stood there looking around, tossing the keys in his hand before setting them on the desk. He fingered the envelope she'd addressed to Rye, then left it alone.

Re-creating the last few minutes they'd spent in the room, he sat on the sofa and looked straight ahead at the desk. To the right stood the wooden file cabinet. To the left, a modern grandfather clock.

Time? Had she been worried about the time? She'd rushed both of them out fast, while he had wanted to linger a bit, maybe learn her last name.

Her name. His gaze riveted on the file cabinet. She'd known Rye for years—not intimately—and she'd left him a note. This was business. Personal business. Rye owned his own investigation firm, had for years. That was how Patrick had met him, when Rye had taken occasional assignments for him. The last assignment Patrick arranged had resulted in Rye's marriage to Paige.

Patrick blinked, bringing himself back to his goal. Jasmine had been sitting facing the desk, facing the file cabinet. Facing the *open* file cabinet. And she had business with Rye.

He retrieved the key from the wall safe and unlocked the cabinet. Slowly he pulled open the drawer marked H-L. Not sure what he was looking for, he started at the front, deciding to make a cursory pass through the folders in search of anything obvious, then a more detailed inspection as necessary.

Toward the back of the cabinet he found it. LeClerc, Jasmine. He pulled the folder halfway out, then stopped. Turning his back on it, he shoved his hands into his pockets, walked to the window and opened the shutters, but the sun had moved higher and no longer flooded the room. Ah, but she'd looked incredible in the sunshine. An earth mother, a siren—an amazingly responsive, giving woman who kept her own confidences well.

As did he.

He turned and looked at the file drawer. He believed in going after what he wanted—if he hadn't, he wouldn't have succeeded in a business where so many others had failed. Privacy had never been a big issue with him because he'd never had much to hide, until recently. But he'd never let anyone see his weaknesses.

Moral dilemmas. He wasn't good at sorting them out. He reacted from the gut most of the time. Sometimes it backfired. More often, it yielded him measurable results. But that was business. This wasn't.

He returned to the cabinet and pulled the file free. As if in slow motion, he moved to the desk, laid the file there

and sat down. He rested his hands on the folder, palms
flat, fingers spread, and took a deep breath. He turned the
page.

Fifteen minutes later, Patrick closed the folder and
rested his head in his hands. She had two children—a son,
Matthew, age fourteen, and a daughter, Raine, age twelve.
Her ex-husband had taken them—stolen them—six years
ago during his weekend visitation. For a while she had
searched on her own. After the first few unsuccessful
months, Rye had gotten involved. And he'd gotten close
several times. Twice, he'd even talked to the man, Deacon
LeClerc. Once by phone, once in person. The children were
nowhere to be found, apparently well hidden in a private
school somewhere in Europe. LeClerc, who came from a
wealthy New Orleans family, could afford to buy seclu-
sion for the three of them and had done just that.

Patrick lifted his head and slumped in the chair, staring
at the ceiling. She was a mother. A mother without children. According to notations in the file, she'd spent
thousands of dollars searching for them before Rye started
charging her a token fee, telling her he was combining the
search with other jobs. But the truth was also in the file—
Rye had spent more of his own money to locate them.

He'd admired his son-in-law for years. The kind gesture to the distraught, deprived Jasmine only sealed Patrick's relief that Paige had him in her life, for the
remainder of her life.

On the other hand, if Rye couldn't get Jasmine's children back, who could? No one human. Patrick could buy
the services of a hundred investigators, but it wouldn't be
quantity that made the difference.

He returned the folder to its place and slammed the
drawer shut. It felt so good, he did it again. And again. He
pulled all four drawers out and slammed them, one at a
time, each time with more force. Then he did it again. And
again. Finally out of breath, he leaned his hands against

LAY

SILHOUETTE'S®

HEARTS

TIME

YOU GET

BOOKS

E GIFT

MUCH MORE

E PAGE AND
URSELF IN

PLAY "LUCKY HEA
AND YOU GET. . .

★   Exciting Silhouette® n

★   Plus a Simulated Pear

THEN CONTINUE
LUCKY STREAK W
SWEETHEART OF

1. Play Lucky Hearts as instructed

2. Send back this card and you'll r
   Silhouette Desire® novels. The
   £2.30 each, but they are yours t

3. There's no catch. You're unde
   We charge nothing for your firs
   to make any minimum number

4. The fact is thousands of reader
   from the Reader Service, at lea
   available in the shops. They li
   delivery, and there is no extra

5. We hope that after receiving
   remain a subscriber. But the
   cancel, anytime at all! So wh
   no risk of any kind. You'll be

the cabinet and hung his head, sucking in air, ignoring his thundering heart.

After a minute, he straightened, shoving his hands through his hair as he looked at another locked cabinet. The file noted several audiotapes made during Rye's interviews with Jasmine, but he wasn't tempted by them. He didn't want to hear her cry. He didn't want to hear her being stoic, either.

The envelope on the desk was a temptation he couldn't resist, however. He ripped it open and read the contents, guilt over his intrusion into her privacy not surfacing through his rage at the injustice.

Rye—
Monica called. Deacon is in England. She thinks she'll be able to pinpoint a location within the next couple of weeks. I'll let you know as soon as I hear from her.
                                                        Jasmine

Patrick recalled the name Monica from the file—a family friend of Deacon's parents who passed information to Jasmine as she gleaned it. Unfortunately, most of the time it was too late. LeClerc had usually moved on.

Patrick sealed the note in a new envelope and did a fair imitation of Jasmine's handwriting to write Rye's name across the front. He shoved the ripped envelope in his pocket. He returned everything to its place and let himself out the front door, where he stood for a full thirty seconds before he climbed into the car.

Now what? Dammit, now what? This changed everything. Everything.

"Find out what's going on with him," Jasmine ordered her sister late that night.

"Me? Why me?"

"Because he might tell *you.*"

Maggie smiled as she rested a hip against the worktable in the kitchen and watched Jasmine set a slice of cheesecake on a layer of strawberry puree. "And he wouldn't tell you if you asked?"

"I don't know. He's been acting really weird ever since he got here. I can't figure him out at all."

"Weird, how?"

Jasmine gestured bewilderment with her hands. "He hasn't asked me to go out with him after work. He hasn't tried to keep me at his table talking. He's acting like...like a customer!"

"That *is* serious."

"Don't tease, Magnolia. I don't know what to think."

Maggie fanned a sliced strawberry on top of the cheesecake while Jasmine dished up some apple pie and added a scoop of vanilla ice cream. "All I know for sure is that my wedding dress fund is starting to look pitiful. One lousy quarter last night and none tonight," Maggie said.

"You're not going to help me, are you?"

"Not. Definitely not."

Jasmine set the desserts on a tray, added forks and a silver coffee server, then started to leave. Her back pressed to the swinging door, she glanced at her sister, who stood there looking supremely smug. "J.D. and I had a nice talk about you last night."

Maggie straightened. The smile fell from her face. "You stay out of it, Jazz. You don't know anything."

"I know what he thinks about you."

"What?"

She smiled and pushed the door open, leaving Maggie sputtering.

Jasmine served the desserts and coffee to the couple celebrating the birth of their first grandchild, then she moseyed to Patrick's table.

"More coffee?" she asked, eyeing the papers spread across the table.

"Yeah, thanks."

He didn't even look at her. She had become a waitress to him, nothing more. The stark change made her suspicious. It was too sudden, too complete. Had he seen her file in Rye's office? Had he read it?

"What are you working on?" she asked as she watched his face carefully for any nuance of change.

"Hmm? Oh, a contract with a Russian firm. I negotiated it, so it's hard for anyone else to step in and take over."

"I didn't realize you were working while you were here."

Patrick smiled to himself. He'd pretty much ignored her all night. Oh, he'd been courteous enough, but not familiar, not pushy, not even seemingly interested. He had caught on to her in Rye's office this afternoon—she didn't like being pressured, but she didn't like being ignored, either. He knew he couldn't let on that he'd learned her secrets, so he'd decided to keep it light between them for now. She was responding perfectly.

Round five—Patrick, by a wide margin.

"I guess the job's in my blood," he said. "I've delegated a lot of my work, but not this project. This one I worked too long and hard to get."

She fingered a crease on the tablecloth.

He followed the movement with his eyes then looked up. "Something on your mind, Jasmine?"

She hesitated. "I guess not."

He tossed down his pen and stretched. "You can tell me. We're friends, aren't we?"

She winced. She definitely winced.

"You haven't asked me out."

She said the words in rapid fire, then took a deep breath. He tried to look unaffected.

"There's only so much rejection a man can take. You asked me to stop seeking you out. I'm cooperating."

"But . . . what about . . . today? In Rye's office." Her cheeks flushed as he lifted his brows questioningly. "On the couch."

He shrugged. "Right time. Right place."

"Oh." She turned and walked away.

Patrick watched her braid swing, remembering how her hair felt as it had drifted across his skin while she'd massaged his back. Feathery. Soft. Tempting. He stared at the papers in front of him, seeing nothing but a blur.

Just about the time he'd focused on the words again, she returned.

"Are you telling me you've stopped pressuring me to go out with you?" she asked.

"That *is* what you wanted. Right?"

"Yes. Yes, of course. You're acting differently tonight. I just wanted to make sure what's going on here."

"Did you change your mind, Jasmine?"

"No. I really think it's for the best."

He watched her finger the cloth again, a telltale gesture he was glad she wasn't aware of. "But if you change your mind," he told her, "you can ask *me* out."

She contemplated his words. "How long are you staying on?"

"That's the big question mark, isn't it?"

She swallowed. "Do I have your word of honor that you won't pressure me?"

"I've sealed a lot of deals just with a handshake. I've never broken my word." He extended his hand.

Jasmine stared into his eyes as she slipped her hand within his grasp. He didn't know, she decided. He was too casual. Relieved, she relaxed.

"That's not to say if another opportunity like today came along, I wouldn't take advantage of it," he said as she pulled her hand away. "I'm no fool."

She stared hard at him. "Neither am I."

* * *

"I took you to the hospital and I picked you up, Patrick. I talked to your doctor, and I know what his orders were. At least six weeks, he said—no work. I am not going to the office for you today. Anyway, it's Sunday."

"It'll take you fifteen minutes, Bill. Fax me the weekly managers' updates for the last month," Patrick said, knowing he was better off ordering than pleading with his secretary of twenty-three years. He tipped the telephone receiver closer to his mouth. "And the last quarter P and L's."

"No. You tricked Mr. Abrahamson's secretary into sending you the Russia contracts. Everyone knows now that they are not to send anything unless I clear it first. You can't make up your own rules this time."

Patrick pictured her, seeing narrowed eyes and pursed lips. Billie Jean Jacoby looked as tough as she sounded. The sixty-three-year-old woman with iron gray hair and orthopedic shoes ran his business like a military operation. He'd seen her cry only once—after her husband's funeral fifteen years ago. Childless and widowed, she'd devoted every day of her life to O'Halloran Shipping.

"Who's the boss here?" he asked.

"I think we both know the answer to that one, *sir*."

"Yeah, you," he said with a chuckle.

"Now that we've got that cleared up—how are you, Patrick?"

"Almost a hundred percent."

A moment of silence, then, "If you're admitting to almost, you must not be ready to come back."

He hesitated, then gave in, needing to tell someone about Jasmine. "Not because of health reasons."

"Ah-hh. I like the sound of that. So, is she beautiful?"

"Indescribably so."

"Nice?"

"That's one part of her. There are more layers than she lets me see. I'll let you know."

"Young?"

"You'd approve, Bill. We're in the same decade."

"Feisty?"

"She's getting there. She tiptoed around me for a while. But she's livened up lately."

"Good. Um, Patrick?"

Hesitance? From Billie Jean? "What?" The word was layered with suspicion.

"About your coming back to the office..."

"I don't think I want to hear this."

"I told you when you merged the two companies that I didn't want a bigger work load."

"Has it increased? You never said—"

"It's just that since you've been gone, and I've had weekends to myself for the first time in all these years, I realized how much I like it." She sounded regretful, but also determined.

"What are you saying, Bill?"

"I really wanted to tell you when you came back, but since you're not in a hurry to get back here... Well, hell." She drew a deep breath. "I'm ready to retire. My sister has a condo in Florida. She's asked me to live with her. She says there are a lot of available men...and if I wait until I'm much older— Well, you know."

Someone must have slugged him. He slumped over the desk and pressed a hand to his stomach. O'Halloran Shipping without Billie Jean Jacoby? He couldn't picture it. With all the changes he'd gone through recently, he'd also have to break in a new secretary? Someone who didn't know his likes and dislikes, who couldn't anticipate his next move? Someone who might expect him to be in a good mood all the time or try to make him weak coffee— or worse, flavored? His job just got ten times harder.

"When do you want to leave?" he asked, trying to keep his voice upbeat. He heard shuffling, as if she'd been holding herself still, waiting for his reaction, then finally relaxing.

"I'll start looking for a replacement. I wouldn't leave until she's completely trained—"

"I know." God, he wanted to cry. He just wanted to lay his head down on the desk and bawl.

"Thank you for making it so easy for me."

He clenched the telephone receiver, fighting against saying words that would make her feel guilty about her decision. "I love you, Bill," he said instead. "Without you, I wouldn't be the man I am. Without you, the business wouldn't exist. Do you think I've forgotten the times you took out personal loans to help us meet payroll when I couldn't get another loan to save my soul? You're entitled to enjoy the rest of your life."

"We accomplished a lot together," she said, her voice gruff.

"We sure as hell did. And I know there's a man out there who'd love to be bossed around a little."

"I'm a pussy cat when I'm in love."

He laughed. "I can't picture it."

"Oh, I can purr with the best of 'em."

When Patrick hung up the phone a minute later, he pushed his hands through his hair and rested his elbows on the desk. He needed to talk to Jasmine. And the club would be closed until Tuesday night. How was he going to pass the days?

Golden Gate Park teemed with people and activity. Patrick heard it all, but his eyes were focused on the ground as he sat on the park bench, his arms propped on his knees.

"You look like you just lost your best friend."

He straightened and found J. D. Duran in jogging gear, dripping with sweat. J.D. watched Patrick intently, his dark eyes asking questions he wouldn't ask out loud.

"May I?" J.D. asked between quick breaths, indicating the seat beside Patrick.

When Patrick motioned in the affirmative, J.D. sat on the park bench. He lifted the hem of his tank top and mopped his brow.

"You're right. I have lost my best friend," Patrick said, still mourning Billie Jean's news of an hour ago. He thought that going for a drive would chase away the blues. With the top down on the convertible, he'd driven without direction until he'd seen the sprawling park and decided to stop.

"Can I help?"

"Know a good secretary?"

J.D. leaned back and raised his face to the sun, closing his eyes and drawing a couple of deep breaths. "Sometimes worse than replacing a wife, I understand. I wouldn't know, of course, since I've had neither."

"And I've had the best of both."

That brought J.D.'s head down. "You're married?"

"Widowed. But she's been irreplaceable."

J.D. folded his arms across his chest and relaxed again. "Good women are hard to find."

Patrick cocked his head. "I don't think that's true. I just haven't been interested."

"Until now."

J.D. bounced his legs, keeping the muscles warm. His eyes were still closed, his face tilted to soak up the sun's rays. Patrick watched him for a minute before he considered how odd it was that they were sharing the bench and conversation as equals. There was nothing of the maître d' in J.D.'s stance or language.

Patrick hadn't been able to fit J.D. into that role in the weeks he'd known him, anyway. His sometimes formal language seemed a pretense, as if he were playing a role. And just like Maggie's drawl thickened on occasion, so did J.D.'s words become more precise—particularly around Maggie.

There was mystery surrounding the man—and an element of danger.

Almost snapping his fingers, Patrick finally made the elusive connection. J.D. reminded him of Rye.

"What agency do you work for?" Patrick asked casually.

J.D. roused himself to yawn and stretch. "Agency?"

"FBI? CIA? Some fringe element the general public isn't aware of?"

He glanced sideways at Patrick. "I am the maître d' at the Carola, a prestigious job for someone of my background."

"I understand you can't tell me. But tell me this much, is Jasmine in danger?

J.D. didn't blink. "To my knowledge, no one at the club is in any kind of danger. Do you know something I don't?"

Satisfied, Patrick abandoned the topic. "What do you mean by 'someone of your background'?"

J.D. watched a man playing Frisbee with his dog. "Limited education and skills. I didn't even speak English until I was almost an adult. My father is from California and I was born here, but my mother is from Mexico. She took me there when I was three. My parents divorced shortly thereafter. My mother told me my father didn't want me."

"Which wasn't true, I gather."

"Far from it, although I believed it as a child, of course. Actually, he'd been told I was dead. Eventually she told me the truth. When I was almost eighteen I found my father."

Patrick's thoughts flew to Jasmine. "What happened?"

"It wasn't easy for either of us. I understood how long and hard my father had searched for me, and the lies my mother had told us both. The adjustment was hard, however. I didn't really know who to trust anymore, so I trusted only myself. Parents who steal their own children do damage that is never fixed, no matter how hard everyone tries." He focused on Patrick. "I have a friend whose children were taken. I've watched what it has done to her, so I know what my father went through. And the government is no help at all. None."

"I know about Jasmine's children," Patrick said quietly, trusting this man who was more than he seemed to be. "She doesn't know that I know."

"It's something she keeps close to her, held prisoner in her heart. She has spoken to me about it only once, when she found out what had happened to me." J.D. looked away. "Since you came, she has been different."

"In what way?"

"Quieter. She is usually quick with her tongue, and cutting. You make her feel different. I think she's afraid of those feelings."

"She isn't alone."

They sat in silence a few minutes longer, then Patrick stood. "Can I give you a lift someplace?"

"No, thanks. I have another five miles to go."

"I'll see you."

"Mr. O'Halloran?"

"Patrick, please."

J.D. nodded, standing, as well, then jogging in place. "Patrick. Have you eaten at the Back Street Diner near your hotel?"

"How do you know where I live?"

He shrugged. "Jasmine mentioned it."

Patrick didn't believe him. "Frankly, I've avoided that particular restaurant. I figured everything would be fried."

"You ought to give it a try. You might be surprised what you find there."

J.D. jogged away, leaving Patrick to contemplate his words.

Ten

—

The Back Street Diner overflowed with life—dishes and pans clattered harmonically, Elvis sang about blue suede shoes on the jukebox, laughter punctuated a steady drone of voices, interrupted occasionally by a shouted demand for more coffee.

Patrick smiled as he glanced around the tiny building, the decor of which probably hadn't changed in thirty years. Red vinyl banquettes, Formica tabletops, chrome-and-vinyl stools at the counter, no-nonsense waitresses wearing starched dusty-rose uniforms and giving the regulars hell. How many places like this had he eaten in? Comfort food in a comforting environment. A place where a second visit constituted family status.

He had come home, even though he didn't know a soul in the place.

"Slumming?" a husky female voice asked from behind him.

He faced the woman who turned him inside out. Correction, he knew one person here. One compact waitress with an efficient walk and curvy body, who wore her uniform well. Too well. It hugged contours he knew intimately and his imagination filled in all the blanks. The tempo of his heart picked up dramatically. "Jasmine," he said, noting her suspicious frown. "What a surprise."

"Is it?"

"I had no idea you worked here."

"Uh-huh. You just happened to drop in." She crossed her arms over her chest. One side of her mouth curved up. "Just your kind of place."

He grinned. *Thank you, J.D.* "I did and it is."

"We don't serve eggs Benedict."

"That's good. I hate 'em. Can I sit anywhere?"

"You're actually going to eat here?"

He felt more than saw the attention they were drawing. A gradual ebb in conversation made Elvis loud enough to seem as if he were there in person, gyrating for the audience of thirty or so in the diner. After a minute, even the clatter of pans stopped. Patrick looked around the room.

"My name is Patrick O'Halloran," he said to the room at large. "I'm new in town. Anyone care to take me under their wing?"

"Patrick," Jasmine cautioned, her voice low and vibrating.

"Over here, Paddy, me boy," a grizzled old man called, patting the stool beside him.

"Are you in Jasmine's section?"

Laughter wheezed from the man sporting days-old stubble. His name had to be Gus, Patrick decided. He looked like a Gus. A retired carpenter, maybe. Or plumber.

"Miz Jazzy holds court on the left side of the room. Miz Star pesters the poor souls on the right."

"Watch your mouth, old man," the skinny, redheaded waitress fired back. "I'll sic Abigail on you."

The man put the back of his hand to his forehead and pretended to swoon. "Not Abigail! Anybody but Abigail!" Laughter followed his dramatic denial.

People introduced themselves to Patrick as he negotiated his way to the appointed stool. Curiosity gleamed in their eyes; genuine welcome was transferred in their handshakes and smiles. Definitely home.

"Derek Edward Shumacher the Fourth," the old man said as they shook hands, his rheumy blue eyes shimmering.

"'The Fourth,'" Patrick repeated.

"Former president of Gold Security Bank."

"Gold Secur—" Patrick shook his head. Boy, had he pegged the man wrong.

"Don't believe me?"

"Does it matter?"

The man cackled and slapped Patrick on the back. "Jazzy, me love, bring this charming fellow some coffee."

"Coming right up, Gus."

"Gus?" Patrick queried.

"That's what they call me. No one knows about the other, you see. And they all think I spent my life working the docks. Mum's the word, right?"

Patrick grinned, understanding Gus had been playing a joke on him. He followed Jasmine's path as she wove her way toward him, refilling coffee as she went, decaf in one hand, regular in the other, then she slipped behind the counter and approached him.

Knowing his choice was decaf, Jasmine poured from the orange-lipped carafe into his cup. "What can I get you?" she asked as she served him. She avoided looking at his face, sure it would still hold a wide grin.

"What's the specialty?"

After she'd put the carafes back on the warmers, she eased a hip against the counter. "Sugar, we don't have specialties," she answered with what she hoped was a condescending lift of her brows. She didn't like him sharing this environment with her, where she was at home and he seemed so out of place in his jeans and three-hundred-dollar sweater. She shoved a menu his way. "We serve breakfast all day, so we have bacon, sausage, ham, eggs and country-fried potatoes. We have pancakes swimming with butter and syrup. We have tuna salad sandwiches and potato chips. We have half-pound cheeseburgers that come with a mound of french fries and onion rings. Everything is loaded with fat and tastes like heaven."

"'Sugar'?" he repeated, latching on to the first word, the one intended to put him in his place.

His grin pierced her. No man should look so boyishly appealing and so devilishly attractive at the same time. Unbidden, memories of the night they'd tried to make love flashed through her. He had, indeed, made love with a slow hand and hot need, just as she had guessed he would. What would it be like to actually have him—

"I'll take a bowl of chili," he said, closing the menu and passing it to her.

"You want a salad with that?"

"Sure."

"What kind of dressing?"

"Surprise me."

"Got your eye on her, have you?" Gus asked as she moved away.

"Mind your own business, Gus," Jasmine called.

"Your business has always been mine, Miz Jazzy," he called back.

What is he doing here? Jasmine wondered. How had he found her? She didn't believe he'd just happened by. In fact, she'd seen him walk past several times over the weeks he'd been in town, and she'd always held her breath, waiting for him to come in. He hadn't even seemed to notice the building.

She tossed some lettuce and other vegetables together before drizzling ranch dressing over it all. She gave him a quick glance, then studied him more closely as she saw he'd been diverted by lively conversation with a few of her regulars. He'd lost weight since the first day she'd seen him, weight he couldn't afford to lose, probably from hiking all over the city as well as the low-calorie meals he ate at the Carola. She added a little more dressing and extra croutons.

His body had been perfect to start with, not in need of any more exercise or any less weight. His shoulders were appealingly broad, his chest and arms well-defined, his legs long and sturdy, his abdomen flat. He had the perfectly tapered body of a gymnast. He'd carried her over the threshold of the honeymoon cottage as if she weighed nothing, and she was no lightweight. For a forty-seven-year-old man—for a *thirty*-seven-year-old man—he was in darn good shape. And he hadn't allowed her any modesty or hesitance either. She'd felt sexier with him than ever in her life. She flashed on an image of him at sixty and her kneeling on a bed still admiring him after all those years, waiting for him to come to her, his hot, needy gaze coveting and admiring her in return.

She shook her head, dispelling the fantasy. Where had that come from? Some repressed wish of a woman newly awakened to lovemaking after long years without? Or the wish of woman who wanted just one man? This man.

She set the salad in front of him, as well as a basket of garlic bread that he hadn't ordered. "What do you hear from Paige and Rye?" she asked.

"Enjoying the Cayman Islands, even though they're working. It's a tricky job, I gather, and they have to take it slowly. They don't think they'll be home for a while yet."

"Rye?" Gus interjected. "That big fellow that looks like some *per*fessional wres'ler?"

"My son-in-law," Patrick said, then bit into a piece of garlic bread. "How do you know him?"

"Do you want your chili now or after your salad?" Jasmine asked.

"After," he answered.

"That big guy, he used to come in here a lot. Was sniffing around Miz Jazzy for a while there."

"How about some cherry pie—my treat?" Jasmine asked Gus cheerfully.

"Don't you go distractin' me, missy. Paddy here asked me a question. I'm intendin' on answerin' it."

"Then no cherry pie." She turned and started to walk away.

"Miz Jazzy?"

Jasmine faced Gus and he turned an imaginary key at his lips, then pretended to throw the key away.

"You want that pie heated?"

"If you could also swing a scoop of that there vanilla ice cream, I'd be most obliged."

Jasmine smiled as she fixed the pie. Gus wouldn't tell Patrick anything else. He was loyal to her. But jealousy had flared in Patrick's eyes, and she welcomed it. There hadn't been anything between her and Rye except friendship—she'd told Patrick as much. But she understood unreasonable jealousy, because she was jealous of his late wife and all the years they'd shared. He was a man who inspired dreams.

Patrick chewed his lettuce automatically and watched her work. His gaze traveled down to her feet, clad in comfortable, well-soled shoes, and back up again, more slowly. She leaned into the ice-cream freezer to scoop out Gus's ice cream and the fabric of her uniform stretched across her derriere and lifted up a little, revealing an inch of lace trim on her slip. Unexpectedly, arousal hit him full force. He was so turned on by Jasmine in her uniform he couldn't even carry on a conversation with the old guy sitting next to him.

"We just think the world of her."

"Huh?" Patrick said, adjusting the napkin in his lap and turning his gaze on Gus.

"Miz Jazzy. She's got a real good heart, that one. We keep tryin' to bring nice young fellows in here, but she don't want nobody. It's sad. Real sad. Lady like that. Shouldn't be alone."

"Nobody should be alone," Patrick said.

"'Cept maybe Abigail. My, don't that look dee-licious," Gus said, smacking his lips as Jasmine set his dessert bribe in front of him then swept the empty salad plate away from in front of Patrick.

She came back in a minute with his chili. "More bread?"

"This is great, thanks." He avoided looking at her. Now that his mind—and other parts of his body—were totally focused on how sexy she looked, he couldn't shake the image. Her skin would seem doubly soft after the starched finish of fabric. The thought of peeling off the uniform and finding her wearing something lacy made his head spin. The thought of removing those garments one by one made his loins pound. Sweat beaded on his forehead.

"Hot stuff, huh?" Gus asked as he scooped a mound of cherry pie and vanilla ice cream into his mouth.

"Ah, um—"

"The chili, Paddy, me boy. The chili."

"Oh, right. Yeah. It's spicy, all right."

Gus's cackle told him he'd seen right through him.

"So, who's this Abigail everyone lives in fear of?" he asked Gus.

"The Wicked Witch of the West," Gus grumbled.

"She doesn't like you, huh?"

"She wants to marry up with me."

Patrick straightened in surprise. "A prospect you don't share?"

Gus took on a dreamy expression. "I was married once. Long time ago. She was a pretty little thing, all soft and cuddly. Pretty blond curls and china blue eyes. Haven't met no woman who could hold a candle to her."

"Don't you think you're cheating yourself by—" Patrick stopped abruptly. Who was he to give advice about giving up ghosts? Hadn't he held Priscilla up on a pedestal to which no other woman could rise? Paige had accused him once of deifying her memory. He'd thought a lot about that lately. And had found himself guilty. A stark impression of himself at Gus's age imprinted itself on his brain. Alone. A handful of friends from a diner his only company. Is that what he wanted for himself? Is that what he was setting himself up for? "So what's this Abigail like?"

"Pretty enough." He grinned. "Pretty old. Pretty mean. And pretty bossy. She'll be in soon. You'll see."

Out of self-preservation, Patrick ignored Jasmine as much as possible. She responded as usual by paying him more attention. He couldn't win either way. After a while, a petite, elegant woman of an age somewhere between sixty and eighty appeared through the front door, then hardly disturbed the air as she moved across the restaurant to sit beside Gus, her back straight as a model's, her hair beauty-parlor fresh.

"Good day, Augustus."

"How many times do I have to tell you, woman? My name is Gus. Not Augustus, not Gustave, or any other of those fancy-schmancy names. Just plain Gus."

Patrick watched their interplay curiously. But the picture of himself old and alone superimposed itself. He didn't want to end up like that.

He watched Jasmine laugh with another customer, then, as if she couldn't help herself, she turned toward him, still

smiling. Her gaze softened for the briefest of moments, or
was he imagining it? He listened to Gus taunt the woman
he assumed was Abigail, heard her answer him in kind in
a voice neither frail nor tentative, and he came starkly
aware of his solitary life.

Picking up the check, he moved toward the cash register. Jasmine walked parallel to him until they faced each
other across the old-fashioned machine.

"Keep the change," he said.

She glanced at the bills, looked ready to argue with him,
then changed her mind. "Thanks."

Lord, she turned him on like no one he'd ever known.
He leaned across the clunky silver-painted cash register,
tipped up her chin with his thumb and forefinger and,
watching her the whole time, kissed her in front of everyone, staking his claim—a brief kiss, nothing intended to
arouse, but still a mark of ownership. Hoots and hollers
echoed in the building. Round six—Patrick.

"Jazzy's got a boyfriend. Jazzy's got a boyfriend." The
chant picked up volume and enthusiasm as Patrick and
Jasmine stared at each other. He waited for her to get an-
gry.

Her lips curved mischievously. "Thanks, sugar," she
said, her eyes sparkling.

"For?"

"Now they'll all stop bringing in those men with great
personalities to meet me. I can play off this for years, since
you live out of town. They know I'm the kind of woman
who'd be faithful, no matter how far away you live."

"Is that so?"

Jasmine tried to interpret the speculative gleam in his
eye. She thought she'd turned the tables nicely. How was
he turning them back?

"I'm a one-woman kind of man myself. Three miles or
three thousand, it wouldn't matter."

Was that panic or excitement that just surged through her body? "I don't want a long-distance affair with you, Patrick."

"So come home with me."

Never. She could never leave San Francisco. It was her only hope left, that her children would somehow find her. She hadn't changed her name, even though she hated the name LeClerc, and she hadn't unlisted her phone number. It was her one chance. Her only chance.

"I have to get back to work," she said.

"Think about it, Night Flower," he said softly. "Just think about it."

She watched him leave and knew she had to put on a show for her friends—either blush or boast.

Neither option suited her mood.

Eleven

———

Jasmine heard Patrick before she saw him. He'd been up-stairs playing cards since eight o'clock, right after he'd finished eating dinner, a routine he'd developed over the past two weeks. He came into the Carola for dinner, car-ried on a how-was-your-day kind of conversation with her, then off he went, either to play poker or billiards. Around eleven-thirty he'd make his way downstairs, give her a thumbs-up and a grin if he came out a winner or a shrug if he lost, complain about the cigar smoke, hang around a minute or two, then he'd leave, his expression never re-vealing whether he was disappointed that she hadn't made an attempt to change their relationship. He was chipping away at her resolve without using any overt tactics.

The routine continued at eleven-thirty each morning when he would stop in at the diner, eat lunch with Gus and the rest of the gang, linger an hour or so, kiss her good-bye, then leave. He made her laugh, gave her looks that said he wanted her, but he'd never broken his word—he hadn't asked her out again.

Tomorrow was Sunday, which meant that after her lunch shift, she wouldn't see him until Tuesday night. The thought terrified her.

She stepped into the foyer as he reached the bottom of the stairs. His hair looked as if he'd run his fingers through it several times. He was laughing.

He spotted her and angled away from the two men who had descended the stairs with him. "Thanks for the pass," he said, looking back and patting his shirt pocket. "I'll see you Monday. You guarantee me a no-hitter, right, Bobby?"

Bobby Vanderkellen, ace pitcher for the San Francisco Giants, strutted a few steps. "I promise to give a better performance than ol' Deadeye here did today. He couldn't hit the toilet with his own—"

Deadeye McGraff shoved his teammate. "There's a lady present."

"Sorry, Jazz," Bobby said instantly. "Didn't see you."

"Now there's a compliment to add to my collection," Jasmine remarked.

"Aw, Jazz, I didn't mean anything by it."

"Obviously."

Bobby and Deadeye followed Patrick to where Jasmine stood, arms crossed over her chest. She tried to keep the sparkle from her eyes, and tapped her foot instead.

"How come you're givin' this guy—" Bobby hitched a thumb toward Patrick "—all those pretty smiles? I've been wantin' one of those for years. The most you gave me was a hard time."

"Maybe 'cause this guy doesn't have a wife, four incredibly beautiful children, and a chauvinistic attitude."

Bobby bowed his head. "You wound me, Jas-meany. You truly do. Tell me honest, though. What's this guy got that I don't?"

"Class?"

Bobby flung an arm around Deadeye's shoulder as they doubled over and laughed before they took turns pushing each other toward and out the front door. Jasmine glanced at Patrick, who looked a little sheepish.

"We had a contest tonight to see who could come up with the raunchiest joke," he explained with a grin. "I won. Bobby gave me a pass to the game on Monday. Thought I'd take Gus."

Something warm pierced her at about heart level, then danced quickly to her nether parts. Kindness was a rare quality, an attractive quality, in her book. Combined with his other attributes that she'd tried so hard to ignore, it was the final nudge. She'd been building toward trusting him for weeks. It was time to take a chance. It was time for some honesty.

"Patrick?"

His eyes shimmered. "Yes, Jasmine?"

"Would you like to go out with me?"

The smile that followed was slow and devastating. "I'd like that very much."

"Tomorrow? After I get off work at two?"

She watched him lift a hand as if he were going to stroke her cheek, then he glanced around and let his hand fall. She'd almost felt his touch.

"I've been patient a long time, Night Flower. Suddenly, I'm too anxious to wait."

"If we went out tonight, I'd probably fall asleep on you..." Her words faded as he grinned.

"Psst, Jazz." Maggie leaned around the corner. "I've got six orders for designer coffees and dessert. If you're done flirtin', I could use some help."

Jasmine nodded. "I'll see you tomorrow, then," she said to Patrick.

"Anything in particular you'd like to do?"

"Except for the time you took me home after we met at Rye's, I haven't been for a ride in a convertible since I was a teenager."

"You're on." Patrick watched her walk away and resisted the temptation to jump up and down cheering. He'd almost given up. He'd come *this* close to going back to Boston, but something in her eyes held him there day after day. He shrugged into his jacket so that he could begin his vigil outside.

"I will be walking her home tonight. You don't need to worry."

Patrick turned toward J.D., who had come up silently beside him.

"Meaning?" Patrick queried.

"Meaning you can go home instead of waiting to know if I'm seeing her safely to her apartment."

"How did you—"

"Why do you think I let her go home alone at all lately? I know you are there behind her, watching, guarding."

Patrick nodded as he relaxed. "I'm curious why you walk her home but not Maggie."

J.D. stiffened slightly. "Maggie does not need me." He paused, then added, "She drives."

"Ah."

"Ah? What does that mean?"

Patrick grinned. J.D. thought he was a closed book. "Just ah. Nothing. Everything."

The Back Street Diner had never seen such flair, Jasmine thought as she watched Patrick step through the door. He wore a blue chambray shirt, aged jeans, and a rust-colored suede vest. He'd hooked a finger under the label of his well-worn brown leather jacket, letting it dangle down his back. He looked casual, sophisticated, self-confident and . . . edible. She swallowed.

She tried to smile when he winked at her and took a seat next to Gus, tossing his jacket on the stool beside him.

"You're late," Gus announced.

"I had some shopping to do." He reached into his shirt pocket and pulled out the contents to wave in front of Gus's face. "How about you go with me to the Giants' game Monday night?"

Gus swiped the moving target out of Patrick's hand. "No foolin'?"

"I never joke about baseball, Gus." He bowed his head. "It's my religion."

"But this is . . . This is some kind of pass or somethin'."

Jasmine stood in front of the two men, intending to fill Patrick's coffee cup.

"I haven't been to a game in, Lord, years and years," Gus said in wonder. "You sure you want to take *me?*"

"Only if you want to sit in a private box, eat hot dogs until you're sick, and meet the players in the clubhouse afterward. How about if I pick you up here at four? We'll watch batting practice first."

"Hoo-eee! A private box. If that don't beat all!" Gus slapped Patrick on the back then went table to table showing off the pass to his friends.

"Thank you," Jasmine said softly. "He doesn't have family, or anyone."

"He could have Abigail, if he wanted."

"The fun for Gus is in keeping her dangling. He's going to give in one of these days. What would you like for lunch?"

"Something without onions?"

He'd asked it as a question, but she decided he was trying to determine her expectations for the day. She watched him move the salt and pepper shakers a few inches to the left.

"I'm nervous," she said quietly, deciding that he was, too.

"Are you? You always seem so much in control."

"Maybe I'm just good at hiding it."

"No pressure today, Jasmine," he said. "We just enjoy the afternoon together. Whatever happens, happens. I haven't planned a seduction."

She watched him for a minute, then made herself smile as she leaned a hip against the counter, more comfortable with hiding her nerves than letting him see. "Too bad, sugar. I was looking forward to one."

"I'm also adaptable," he said leisurely, letting his gaze drift down her then back up.

"You are one hot number in that outfit you threw together," she told him.

"Yeah? Well, you have no idea how turned on I am by you in that uniform."

Jasmine knew he was telling her the truth—his truth. She knew it from his unwavering stare and the set of his mouth. She glanced at the clock. One hour to go.

It was a big step she was taking, Patrick decided as he watched Jasmine emerge from the rest room at the diner, having changed into a floral-print skirt that skimmed her calves and a bright pink sweater that fell below her hips. She had to walk past all of the regular customers and leave with him. Every one of them would know they were going on an official date. He wondered if any of them had ever seen her in street clothes.

Wolf whistles followed them out the door, the sound carrying even as they climbed into Paige's convertible. Patrick reached behind the seat and brought out a cellophane-wrapped flower.

"This reminded me of you," he said.

Within the crackling paper lay a single white calla lily. She hugged it to her. "Oh, it's lovely. Thank you, Patrick."

He dug behind the seat again and brought out a foil-wrapped open box and passed it to her. "So did this."

She choked on a laugh. "A cactus?"

"Prickly pear," he supplied with a grin, then he brushed his finger along her cheek, over her ear, across her jaw. "You're every flower in between, as well, a different bloom for each mood."

"If you don't kiss me, I'm going to cry."

He granted her request, savoring her heated response and the soft, throaty sounds she made until around them came knocking on the windows, fast and noisy.

"What the—" He jerked back and looked through the windshield, then all around the car. Most of the diner's patrons were there banging on the windows and grinning. "Some friends you've got there, Miss Jasmine."

"Interrupted the high point of my day," she grumbled good-naturedly. "Can we get going?"

He started the car and pushed the button to lower the top. "Show's over, folks," he said.

When the crowd dispersed, only Gus and Abigail remained.

"Sure you can handle him, Miz Jazzy?" Gus asked.

"She looked like she was handling him just fine, Augustus."

"I wasn't talkin' to you, woman."

"I am aware of that. I could handle *you* just fine, Augustus, if you'd give me a chance. I'm a helluva kisser," Abigail announced.

Gus stared at her, dumbfounded. Then he grabbed her, pulled her close and kissed her.

"I'll be damned," he said, touching the back of his hand to his lips when he let her go. "Well, I'll be gol-darned double damned. You *are* one helluva kisser, woman. What do you say we go talk this over a bit?"

Patrick exchanged a look of amazement with Jasmine, then he pulled into traffic before they started laughing.

"Are you warm enough?" he asked after a couple of minutes. The day was beautiful, but typically San Francisco cool, especially in the open convertible. "You could wear my jacket, if you want."

She wriggled in the seat, getting comfortable. "I'm fine. Where are we going?"

"How long has it been since you walked the Golden Gate Bridge?"

"You know, I don't think I ever have."

"Then that's what we're doing."

The open car didn't allow for much conversation as they drove through the city, but words didn't seem to matter. It was enough to be together. They parked near the bridge and sat waiting for the convertible top to come up.

"What brought you to San Francisco?" he asked over the sound of the motor.

She answered before she could let herself clam up about it. "My ex-husband was living here at the time we got married."

"You met him in Louisiana?"

"Yes. I was working at a club similar to the Carola and going to college. He'd been raised there, and had come back to visit his parents." The memories came back full force as the convertible top settled over their heads again. "Deacon pretty much wore me down. I had never wanted to get married. I fought him for a long, long time. My mother has been married six times—or is it seven now?— I can never remember. I haven't met all the husbands. She has always needed a man to take care of her. I don't," she added for good measure.

"I haven't tried to take care of you," he said quietly, shifting toward her.

She mirrored his pose. "You would if I gave you the slightest indication that I wanted you to. Be honest."

"Most men feel that's their role, though. We are the providers, the caretakers, the defenders. I was raised that way." He curved a hand over hers. "Women's movement or no, I still like being the one to provide. But that doesn't mean I wouldn't adapt, just that it's my preference."

"Was your wife a homemaker?"

There was the slightest hesitation. "Yes. But had she wanted to work, I would have supported her decision."

Jasmine smiled, needing to change the subject. "I think being married to you would be a full-time job."

"Really? Why?"

She laughed at his amazed expression. "Sugar, you've got so much energy, it fairly sizzles around you. Keeping up with you would be a challenge. You walk, you pace, you fidget. You drum tunes with your silverware! Sitting still in the booth at the club was driving you crazy. I couldn't figure how you were doing it and staying sane."

"Because I had someone fascinating to watch."

She didn't want to react to his words, but warmth seeped into her like a cup of chamomile tea on a wintry day. "Why haven't you gone home, Patrick?"

"You know the answer to that." He tugged her toward him. "Come on. You're in for a surprise."

Surprise wasn't the word for it. The bridge swayed and rumbled. San Francisco Bay, a terrifying distance below them, was dotted with sailboats and windsurfers skimming over whitecaps created by an unrelenting wind that whipped and swirled so much that it propelled the people on land as well. She clung to Patrick's hand, uneasy with the myriad sensations, the heart-stopping marvels of nature at full force.

Patrick was oblivious to the elements, except to enjoy them. He lifted his face to the wind and smiled, savoring the rush of feeling, the primal connection with life. He felt Jasmine squeeze his hand and was glad she was reacting to the majestic splendor of it all.

"Okay, stop here," he said, turning to face her. "Look up."

She complied, then swayed, her other hand grabbing blindly for him. She brought her head forward quickly. "Oh!"

He locked his hands behind her waist. "I'll support you. Just lean back and look up. Watch the tower sway. Feel the bridge shudder. It's incredible, isn't it? I've never felt anything like it."

Her fingers dug into his arms. "Don't let go of me."

"Never."

Jasmine blinked at the word and shifted her head to make eye contact with him, seeing the hunger in his soul being fed by the experience, filling him with something basic in life he needed. He loved the scary sensations. She was just scared. The differences between them had never seemed so stark.

He stared back at her for an endless second, then lowered his head to hers with a primitive need.

She stopped thinking about differences and keyed in to what he was feeling instead, catching the wildness as it blew a gale force through her. She trusted him enough to luxuriate in the overpowering strength of his kiss, pulling herself closer with a lunge of reaction, ignoring the runners and bikers who zoomed past them, until a couple of teenage boys made exaggerated kissing sounds as they danced around them, becoming generally obnoxious. She didn't want the moment to end, so she burrowed against him and held on tight.

"Have you given any more thought to coming back to Boston with me?" he asked, his voice taut.

She squeezed her eyes shut. "Don't ask me, Patrick. Please. I can't leave here." She pushed back just enough to look at him. "I have something I need to tell you, though. And maybe it will change how you feel about me. But you have to know."

He warmed her ears with his hands; his eyes shimmered with tenderness. "Not here," he said, as if he knew what she was going to say.

"No. Not here. Someplace quiet."

"Your apartment? My cottage?"

"Not somewhere personal."

He looked at her a moment longer. "Okay. I know the place."

The walk back to the car wasn't half as terrifying—maybe because she was focused on what was ahead. She didn't want to lose his respect. She didn't want to lose everything else that had been building, either. It was a lot to risk.

They drove to a spot overlooking the bay, but stay co-cooned within the car. Traffic was sparse behind them. They weren't alone in the world, but they were alone enough.

"It's all right, Night Flower. You can tell me any-thing," he said into her silence.

"No. No, it's not all right. I've de— Oh, I can hardly get the words out." She drew a deep breath, wishing she could keep the secret to herself forever, knowing she couldn't. "I've deceived you. I tried to trick you."

She watched his brow furrow with confusion, as if he hadn't thought her capable of deception.

"Into what?" he asked.

"Impregnating me. I wanted a baby. I picked you to fa-ther it." She said the words in a rush, running them to-gether. Everything inside her quaked. It was an act of pure selfishness telling him the truth now, when nothing could come of it beyond his leaving San Francisco hating her. But the truth mattered more.

She watched his face contort and his body stiffen with reaction. Before her eyes he became a mass of the emo-tion and energy she'd seen in him since she'd met him.

"You lied? You lied about something as important as bringing a child into the world? *My* child?"

"It gets worse."

He stared wordlessly at her, waiting for her explanation.

"I hadn't ever intended to tell you about it."

He turned from her, his jaw clenched, still speechless.

"I'd gone to a clinic first. It was too expensive. I came to the conclusion I needed an anonymous but free, um, donor." This was harder than she'd thought, and she realized how calculating she'd been—and how omnipotent. She'd attempted to play God with three lives.

"You would have gotten pregnant and never told me? You would have denied me my child?" he asked hoarsely, his anger simmering just below the surface.

"It seemed like a good idea. For a while. Before—" She fumbled for answers, hating her halting words and quavery voice, wishing his opinion of her didn't matter so much. "Well, before I'd weighed the human factors into it. I'm glad it didn't work, though, Patrick. It was a foolish idea that I abandoned the morning after we first tried. That's why I left so fast. I learned my lesson, I promise you. I've—" her breath caught "—resigned myself to being alone."

"So, when you came home with me that first night, it was only for the purpose of getting pregnant?"

"I told myself that."

"But?"

She lifted her chin. "But I was there because I thought I could give you something, too. You were grieving. I thought you needed me, too—just for different reasons." She touched his arm, feeling only steely hardness. She let her hand drop away. "But, Patrick, that night is a beautiful memory for me. I don't regret what happened or the outcome. And I value you. I really do."

He turned slowly back to face her, controlled and decidedly cool. "Why do you want a baby so much?"

That much she couldn't share with him. That secret had to stay her own. Oh, she wanted to tell him. For purely selfish reasons, she wanted to confide in him, needing his sympathy and understanding. But every time she talked about Matthew and Raine she lost a little bit of them. After six years of not seeing them, not holding them, her memories had faded so much she had to stretch beyond her conscious mind to find them now. If she gave up even a tiny fragment of memory, they would be lost forever. Forever.

And if she told him her children had been stolen from her, Patrick might think she wasn't worthy of being a mother. She didn't want him to believe that.

"Why does anyone want a child?" she said finally, cautiously, watching him for reaction, seeing something indecipherable cross his face as she clung to her children's fading memories. "You have a daughter you love, who loves you back. You're proud of her. You raised her, watched her grow. I hear how much you love her in your voice when you talk about her. I want—*wanted* that, too."

Patrick controlled his response enough to make Nurse Crackwhip proud of how well he was handling the tumult within. He knew about Jasmine's children only because he'd violated her privacy and read her personal file. He turned to face the windshield, gripping the steering wheel as he came to terms with their mutual deceptions.

He could force the issue by coming clean himself, but what good would that do? He had other secrets, as well, ones he needed to share. And if he did, maybe she would.

"Is that all?" he asked, giving her one last chance, even though he realized how much it had cost her to tell him *this* truth. She hadn't been under any obligation to let him know, not after the fact.

"Isn't that enough?"

He pulled her braid over her shoulder, sorry that she flinched before she realized what he was doing. The last thing he wanted was for her to fear him in any way. "I think we deserve a day of fun, don't you?"

She frowned, her surprise evident. "Yes, but—"

"No buts." He tugged on her hair. "I'd like to show you the San Francisco I've discovered."

Her eyes glistened; she pursed her lips. "Thank you," she said, her voice soft and husky.

"I guess we have a lot to work out," he said. "But it doesn't all have to happen today."

Twelve

"I can't believe that won the raunchiest joke contest," Jasmine said on a laugh as Patrick opened the door to his cottage.

"I might have toned it down just a little." He flicked her braid as she moved past him. "There's a lady present, after all."

She heard the key clatter as he tossed it on the table. She looked around the expensively furnished, immaculate room, grateful that he'd agreed to stop here to pick up a blanket so that they could keep the top down on the car into the night—at least, that was the excuse they were using for why they'd come here. If they each had other ideas, they hadn't yet shared them.

Her gaze lingered on the fireplace. Someone undoubtedly cleaned the hearth and arranged kindling and logs for a fresh fire daily. Money bought convenience.

"Have a seat," Patrick said as he moved past her.

She headed straight to the couch and flopped onto it, sighing heavily. "Oh, it feels good to get off my feet. We must have walked more than ten miles. Do you do this every day?"

"I walk a lot," he said, disappearing into the bedroom.

For almost seven hours they had laughed and teased and touched. It had been leading to this all day, and the anticipation was almost unbearable. Amazingly, he had seemed to slough off her revelation of earlier. At least, he hadn't mentioned it again. At some point today she'd stepped past her fears, because she recognized she'd fallen in love with him—maybe even weeks ago.

She watched him walk toward her, carrying a blanket and an extra jacket, and her heart did a pirouette. His smile stopped her breath in her throat.

Tossing the items on the sofa, he crouched in front of her, wrapping his hands around her ankles. "You've been on your feet for most of the past twelve hours. Would you like a foot rub?"

She nodded, his touch freezing her words as he slid her shoes off.

"Are you hungry?" he asked, pressing his thumbs into her arches.

She shivered in reaction. "A little."

"Should I light the fire? I could order room service instead of us going out."

Her gaze connected with his. "That would be nice."

"Why don't you take off your stockings, or panty hose or whatever. I can give you a better massage." He shifted toward the fireplace and lit a match. The tinder caught instantly. Still crouched, he angled toward her. "What would you like for dinner?"

She was supposed to care about food when he looked at her like that? "Something light," she said.

She was aware of him watching her as she stood and slid her hands under her skirt, catching the elastic waistband of her panty hose then shoving them down and off, enjoying the heat of his gaze as it traveled upward.

"What does your T-shirt say?" he asked. "I can make out letters through your sweater, but that's all."

She peeled the sweater over her head. "It's a promotional gimmick for a local radio station. The morning deejay gave it to me."

KCUP...The Stuff Dreams Are Made Of was emblazoned across her chest. The lacy cups of her new bra abraded her tightening nipples as he read the words.

His eyes lit with humor, and more than a little fire, as he surveyed her chest. "Truth in advertising." He took her sweater as she sat down, laying it neatly aside, adding his vest. After unbuttoning his shirt cuffs, he rolled them up a few turns before sliding his shoes off and setting them beside hers. "I'll call room service—"

Jasmine leaned forward and unbuttoned his shirt, tugging it from his jeans and letting it dangle open. She eased her hands under the loosened fabric and rested them on his chest a minute before letting them wander over him, feeling his warmth. He stilled; the pattern of his breathing changed. He covered her hands with his, then pulled one to his mouth to press a kiss to her palm. She held her breath as he traced her lifeline with his tongue.

"Are you ready for this?" he asked, his voice low and strained.

"I'm ready but—"

He cut off her words with a staggering kiss, pulling her to him, holding her with the strength of his need. "I've wanted you so much," he said. "I can't tell you how much." He tipped her head to the other side and kissed her again, the different angle providing a whole new sensation.

Moaning, she gave herself wholly to him, kissing him back, shoving his shirt off so she could taste the warm, salty skin covering his shoulder. She left a damp trail with her tongue as she followed his collarbones to his other shoulder, letting her hands drop to his belt buckle.

Patrick shifted to give her access, then stopped her wandering hand after she'd lowered his zipper. "Let's do this right. We deserve that." He lifted her into his arms.

"Wait a second," she said breathlessly.

He stopped cold, wondering what surprise she had in store for him now.

She ran a shaking hand through his hair, brushing it back repeatedly. "I haven't taken my temperature since last month. I don't know if— Patrick, we need to use protection."

"I haven't bought any," he said, setting her down reluctantly. "You said I wouldn't need it. There was no reason— What? What's wrong?"

She drew a quavery breath. "Nothing. Nothing. It's just that you hadn't bought any."

"Why would I?" he asked, confused. "You said—"

"I know. But it says so much more than that. You didn't expect to be with anyone else."

"Why the hell would I?"

She pressed her fingers to his lips. "Shh. Don't be mad. It's just that no one's ever made me feel so special. So... cherished. You overwhelm me."

He didn't know what to say to that, so he held her instead. "I'll go to the store," he said at last. "There's one a few blocks away."

"Okay." She stepped out of his embrace and watched as he scooped up his shirt. "Oh, my gosh," she said suddenly. "Wait a second."

She dug her wallet out of her purse and rummaged through it, then triumphantly held up a plastic-wrapped square.

"You—" He swallowed hard as laughter threatened. "You have a condom in your wallet."

"Hey, I'm a woman of the nineties. We come pre-pared."

Patrick examined the packet. "And you've been carry-ing this for how long?"

She shrugged. "Does it matter?"

"It might."

She moved close to him and pressed her mouth to his chest, sweeping his nipple with a light swirl of her tongue. She hooked his open jeans with her hand and tugged. "There's nothing stopping us now. Patrick, please. I've wanted you for so long."

He didn't want to think anymore—not about conse-quences or responsibility or the possibility of failure. He needed her, wanted her. They'd earned this time together.

He kissed her fiercely as he lifted her in his arms again and moved into the bedroom. As soon as he stood her be-side the bed, she leaned over to pull down the bedding. From behind he held her hips, pressing himself against her rear. As she straightened he loosened her T-shirt and lifted it off her. He heaved it aside, then took a calming breath before he cupped her breasts. She moaned his name and leaned against him, his chest a heating pad for her back.

"Night Flower. Jasmine. You are so beautiful, so very beautiful," he told her as he slid a hand under the lacy fabric to mold the soft flesh. Her hard nipple settled in his palm; one bra strap whispered down her arm. He loved the way she squirmed in response. "What do you want? Tell me what you want me to do."

"Just love me, Patrick. Please. Just love me."

"Call me sugar. I like when you call me sugar."

"Sugar," she repeated, but no longer with the teasing tone. It had become an endearment, a word of deep meaning.

He hooked her other strap and sent it down her other arm, pulling on the satin strip until he could see her nip-ples nestled in the fabric. Her breasts were warm and welcoming as he slid his palms over her curves. His fingers curved around the taut peaks, displacing her bra further. With a measured movement, he unhooked the garment and let it drop to the floor.

Patrick closed his eyes as he let her flesh settle in his hands, his thumbs caressing, measuring, teasing, loving as she shuddered, rubbing her head against his chest. He tried to keep it slow and tender. He wanted to throw her across the bed and lunge.

"Don't be gentle," she whispered, somehow sensing his restraint. She guided his hands to the tips of her breasts, closing his thumbs and forefingers over the tight flesh there and squeezing, their hands brushing her flesh at the same time. "I don't need or want gentleness. Patrick, please. Just let yourself go."

"As long as you take the same freedom," he said, urgency overwhelming him.

"I will. I promise you, sugar, I will."

He groaned as he lightly bit the soft flesh of her shoulder. His hands dropped to her waist. He shoved her skirt down, kneeling behind her and tossing the garment aside when she stepped out of it, the soft sounds she made, incoherent and flattering. He followed the elastic trail of her high-cut panties with his tongue down her right buttock, then her left, before he tugged the fragile bit of silk down. He sucked on her flesh, branding her with a sign of his passion, leaving a telltale mark of ownership.

He eased back, giving her the freedom to turn and face him. "Take down your hair," he said, the words scraping his throat as he stood.

Jasmine knelt on the bed, facing him, and pulled her braid over her shoulder, working it free. She combed it with her fingers, shaking her head back and forth so that her hair floated down her back and her breasts swayed.

He made it easy, being so totally exposed to him. His admiration was obvious, his desire evident in the bulge of his unzipped jeans. He'd made her feel sexy from the first moment she'd met him, she realized. He'd always looked at her as if she was perfect, as if every young, firm female body that passed by him wasn't of the slightest interest. But it was more than flattery she felt. Much more.

She rose on her knees and opened her arms to him. He pulled her against him and kissed her fiercely, with a need that came from deep within, matching her moan for moan, touch for touch, taste for taste. He arched her back, settled a knee between hers as he leaned over and tongued her breasts, suckled her nipples, and peppered her flesh with tiny love bites.

"You're a little overdressed," she said, sliding her hand into his jeans.

"Why don't you help me remedy that?"

"My pleasure." Her smile was slow, her movements even slower as she caressed him first, his masculine strength a temptation too strong to resist. She heard his groan and smiled as he closed his eyes. She managed to push his jeans and briefs off together, then they faced each other without anything except secrets separating them. And for now, the secrets didn't matter.

"I want you, Patrick."

It was a kiss that memories were made of—passionate, needy, endless. A kiss that vanished all other memories, incinerating them forever. He pulled her closer, sealing their bodies, his rigid heat pressed against her abdomen, searing her skin, drawing her answering need. She curved a hand around him, feeling his warmth and strength and passion.

"You're everything I've ever needed, Jasmine. You're everything—"

He laid her against the cool sheets. His hot mouth moved over her body with a fervor, touching every known erogenous zone and some she hadn't known qualified as such. Rolling with her, he ended up below her and she returned the favor of putting his erogenous zones to the test. He passed every one.

"Just a second," he said suddenly, seeming to catch his breath.

She backed away to look at him, a question in her eyes.

"I'm all right," he said, as if convincing himself. Confused, she laid a hand against his face, willing him to look at her.

He pressed a kiss to her palm, then retrieved the packet to protect them. In a moment he flattened her against the mattress, covering her instantly with his body.

He nudged her legs wider. She closed her eyes as he hovered at the entrance to her femininity, letting her feel how hot he was, testing her for readiness, as well. Then suddenly he was inside and he was squeezing her within arms of steel. He struggled for air. She could hear the lack of rhythm and the fight to fill his lungs fully. She was about to question him when he started to move, and she forgot everything but sensation....

The feel of him deep within her, the weight of his body, the harshness of his breath against her hair, the distinctive scent of him. He shifted so that he could kiss her, trapping moans that boomeranged back and forth in each other's mouths. She arched high; he pushed deeper, dragging her legs up. Every muscle in her body tightened under the increasing rigidity of his. She yanked her mouth from his to cry out at the stunning explosion within, her fingers digging into his buttocks. She heard him find his own release as he drove relentlessly into her, the rhythm precise until the final few thrusts that held a little longer with each one.

As soon as he collapsed on her she curved her arms over his shoulders and held on tight. He started to shake.

"Patrick? What is it?" She tried to move him, but his full weight lay against her. "Patrick?" Panicked now, her voice rose hysterically.

He shifted off her, fell onto his back and pressed his hands to his face. His entire body shook.

She rolled toward him, her hands fluttering over him. "Patrick, talk to me! Patrick!"

He pulled his hands from his face, revealing the stupidest grin she'd ever seen on a man. "I'm sorry..." Whatever else he intended to say got lost in laughter.

"You're *laughing?*" Horrified, she backed away from him.

"Don't leave," he said between chuckles, throwing a leg over her to prevent her going anywhere.

"I don't want to be near you, Patrick O'Halloran. You're laughing at me!" She couldn't move an inch; he held her easily, but well. She wished for a fraction of his strength so she could haul off and slug him.

"I'm not laughing at you," he said at last. "If anything, I'm laughing at myself. But mostly I'm laughing because I'm happy. That was relief, Jasmine. Pure and utter relief."

She eyed him suspiciously. "What was?"

"You don't know how afraid I was to make love with you. To go all the way. That little problem I had last time?"

"I remember it well."

"I didn't tell you the truth about what was happening to me." He looked into her eyes and smiled. "A couple of weeks earlier I'd had a heart attack."

"A *heart attack?* And you didn't *tell* me?" She struggled to get free. She really wanted—*needed*—to hit him. And *she'd* been worried about keeping secrets from him? And, oh, God... She examined every inch of his face, searching for truths. He could have died. Before she'd even met him. Known him. Fallen in love with him.

"Don't move," Patrick said, struggling to stop laughing. He watched a change come over her, feature by feature. Her eyes filled with tears as she put her hands against his face.

"Are you all right?" she whispered.

He turned his head to kiss her palm. "I'm doing fine."

"Honest?"

He loosened his hold on her. She didn't try to move away. "I know you have little reason to believe me, but it's the truth. The cardiologist tells me it was a minor heart attack. I had very little pain, and no apparent damage to the heart muscle."

"Were you alone? I hope you weren't alone." The worry on her face carried through in her voice.

"My secretary was working late with me. I would have ignored it. She insisted I call my doctor and he insisted I go to the emergency room. Good thing, too."

Her eyes opened wide; she pressed a hand to her mouth. "Oh, my God. You've been on some special diet and exercise program, haven't you?"

"Nurse Crackwhip's Guide to a Healthy Heart."

Her fingers curled into a fist. She spoke through it. "I noticed you'd been losing weight. I've been trying to fatten you up."

He smiled as he brushed the backs of his fingers up and down her cheek. "I know. Thank you."

"But what if it hurt your recovery?"

"I think we can both rest easy about that. I seem to have recovered just fine."

She relaxed against the bed. He massaged her thighs.

"Patrick?"

"Yes, Jasmine?" He loved when she did that—said his name as if the next words she uttered were the most important of her life.

"Why hadn't you— How can I put this delicately?"

"Since when do you need to be delicate with me?"

She cleared her throat. "Well, why hadn't you tried to…well, you know, do it, on your own, to see if it would work?"

He laughed at the blush that spread across her face. "I figured if I was gonna up and die during the last, uh, moment of glory of my life, I wanted it to happen with you."

"Oh, well, thank you so much. I would have loved having you up and die on me in the throes of passion."

"You see why I didn't tell you?" He rolled off the bed. "I'll be back in a minute."

She watched him disappear into the bathroom. When he came out, he had a bemused smile on his face.

"What?" she asked.

He dropped onto the bed beside her. "What, what?" he asked, shifting so that he could draw circles around her nipples with his finger, and he watched as the peaks drew taut and tempting. He tasted her leisurely.

She sucked in a breath. "You look like you know something I don't."

"Do I?" He pulled a pebbled crest into his mouth, the suction steady and demanding.

"Patrick."

"Hmm?"

"You're ignoring me."

"I thought I was doing a damn good job of paying close attention to you."

She gave up. "You didn't even notice my new underwear," she said, shifting as his mouth did exciting, intriguing things to her body.

"I noticed."

"You didn't say anything."

"Pink. Lacy. Skimpy. Powerful." Patrick sucked a little harder, enjoying her squirming reaction, enjoying his own body's response as he grew heavy with need. Enjoying feeling like a whole man again. "And what was underneath those tiny bits of lace was an aphrodisiac." He moved down her body deliberately, tongued her navel, then her abdomen . . . and beyond.

"I'm too. . ." She stopped him from going farther.

"What?"

"You know."

He pressed his lips to her femininity, then moved up to kiss her. "There's a difference between men and women, Night Flower," he said, his lips brushing hers again and again. "The only thing *too* you are is sexy. Don't think about it. Don't think about anything."

"But, Patrick—"

"What?"

"What about you? After all this time, you need it more than I do."

"You think we're gonna run out of steam, Miz Jazzy? I assure you, we've got plenty left. There's something you probably should know, however."

"What?" She arched as he sent his fingers on an intimate foray.

"You failed your test as a woman of the nineties."

She grabbed his hand, stopping his teasing. "What do you mean?"

"Exactly how long had you been storing that condom?"

Confusion and suspicion warred on her face. "Years. I don't know how many. It was just a symbol of my indepen . . ." Her words drifted off.

He laid his hand on her abdomen. "It broke."

She scrambled to an upright position and moved away from him. "Oh, my God! Oh, my God! Patrick! I didn't do it intentionally. I swear to you." She pushed her hair back. "I didn't."

He sat up beside her. Side by side, they leaned against the headboard and stared straight ahead. "I believe you. What do you think the chances are that you could conceive tonight?"

"I don't know." She pulled up her legs and pressed her forehead to her knees. "It's probably too late in my cycle. Plus, given my age, the possibility of it happening on a first attempt diminishes greatly." She lifted her head and looked at him. "Now what? What do we do?"

Now what, indeed? Patrick wondered. "I guess this means I don't have to go to the store."

"I guess not."

He heard the hesitance in her voice. Fate had dealt their hand—they might as well play it out. The thought of not having to use protection after all those years of being cautious appealed to him. More than it should, perhaps. Maybe for reasons he didn't want to acknowledge.

He angled sideways. "I've never been one to waste an opportunity," he said, and watched the tension in her ease. Then he set about proving his words.

Thirteen

———

Patrick awoke with a start, every muscle rigid. Jasmine shifted in his arms. Automatically, he stroked her hair, and she settled against him again, her breathing deep and even. He closed his eyes, but the pain came again. Just a twinge. Maybe just a cramped muscle.

He tried to relax by drawing slow, easy breaths. A few minutes passed without discomfort. He thought about her need to have a child. He thought about the condom that she'd carried in her wallet for too long. He thought about how his wife had gotten pregnant even though he'd used protection. He wondered—

The ache elevated to more than a twinge. Tucking the sheets around her, he slid out of bed, rotating his arms as he moved, seeing if it was just muscle cramps. He wandered into the bathroom, grabbed his robe from the door, then moved into the living room. Nothing. The pain didn't return.

Not taking any chances, he closed the connecting door to the bedroom, then sat at the desk before lifting the telephone receiver and dialing. The call was answered on the second ring.

"Hey, Glenn," he said, and was greeted with a few seconds of silence.

"You know, Patrick, I'd actually gotten used to sleeping a whole night without a call from you. Don't tell me you're finally home."

Patrick smiled at the sound of his lawyer's drowsy voice. Okay, so he'd forgotten it would be 3:00 a.m. in Boston. He had some business that couldn't wait. "Sorry, pal. I'm still in California. I forgot the time." He kept his voice as low as possible.

"So, what's new? What can I do for you?"

"I need to change my will."

"Now?"

"I want you to do something temporary, but something that will hold up in court, and fax it to my daughter's house first thing in the morning."

"Your morning or mine?" Glenn asked dryly.

Patrick laughed quietly. "Mine will do. I'll sign the fax and have it witnessed, notarized, whatever I need to do. Then when I come back we'll do something more detailed."

From the muffled background sounds, Patrick gathered Glenn was finally sitting up in bed. The click of a light followed, then the glide of a drawer being opened and shut.

"Okay, shoot," he said.

"I may have gotten a woman pregnant."

"*What?*"

"If so, I want her to split eighty percent of my estate with Paige."

"And if she didn't conceive the royal heir?"

"That's what I like about you, Glenn. You never resort to sarcasm."

"Just answer the damn question, Patrick."

"If I didn't get her pregnant, she gets twenty percent, although I think she'll turn it down. But give it a shot anyway." He spelled Jasmine's name for him as he rubbed his chest with his hand.

"That leaves twenty percent unaccounted for."

"Billie Jean still gets five. The other fifteen go into a trust to give financial help to parents who have had children stolen by ex-spouses. It would need a board of directors, I think, to make the determinations. Offer the job of chairman to Jasmine. If she turns it down, ask a J. D. Duran. Rye can help you locate him if—well, just *if*."

"What's going on? The Patrick I know would have assigned the job, not asked."

"People change."

"Uh-huh. Will Paige contest this?"

"Paige would be the first one to tell me to spend my money the way I want to. Rye will provide well for her. On second thought, you'd better give Paige forty-one percent and Jasmine thirty-nine. Paige will know what to do with the company. We'll let her make those decisions."

"Okay." There was a long pause, then, "You sound happy, Patrick."

"I had a heart attack. It was the best thing that ever happened to me."

"Damn, but you're full of surprises. Why didn't you tell me?"

"Because—" The bedroom door opened and Jasmine stood there, naked, glorious, tempting. Words jammed in his throat as she rubbed her eyes and walked toward him. His body responded instantly. He tipped the receiver up when Glenn said his name a second time. "I'm sorry I woke you, pal. But you'll take care of everything, right? And if necessary, forge the signature."

"I can't do that."

"Sure you can." Patrick heard Glenn's wife call hello in the background. "Tell Mary Ellen I'm sorry I woke her, too."

Glenn's chuckle came across the wires. "There's one thing about the middle of the night, Patrick. No chance of the kids walking in on us. I'll fax your stuff in the morning."

Patrick cradled the receiver and extended an arm in invitation to Jasmine.

"Who was that?" she asked, shoving his robe aside and straddling his lap. She tossed her hair over her shoulder.

He burrowed his nose between her breasts. They had taken a bath together a couple of hours ago, had played with each other leisurely before he'd hauled her out of the tub and laid her soaking wet and protesting about it on the bed then lunged into her, moving her across the bed a thrust at a time, until her head dangled over the side and he cradled it with his hands. "This is supposed to bring you pleasure beyond your imaginings," he'd told her, shifting her a little farther, until her shoulders arched downward. Her fingers had dug into him.

Then she'd confirmed his supposition vigorously and loudly.

"That was an employee," he said, sniffing her skin, loving the scent.

"In Boston? At this time of night?"

"He's paid to be available."

"Proclaims Lord Patrick..."

Her words drifted as he teased her with his fingertips to see what drew the quickest response.

"Oh, sugar, aren't you worn-out?"

He loved this whole new tone of voice when she called him sugar. It might as well be darling or love or sweetheart. "Are you?"

"Well, no, but..."

He smiled as she closed her eyes. "But?"

"Don't stop." Jasmine tightened her legs against him as he teased her. "I've been so jealous of your wife."

He went absolutely still. "Why?"

She opened her eyes. "I'm sorry. I guess this wasn't the time to bring her up. It's just that I've only had you a short time and she—"

He kissed her with a passion elementally close to violence, a passion she returned wholeheartedly, trying to dispatch the grievous error she'd just made. What an idiotic thing to do, bringing his late wife into their bed. Smart, Jasmine. Real smart. She climbed off his lap and knelt in front of him, looking into his eyes, eyes that glittered. She leaned forward and took him into her mouth, feeling his hands clamp her head, hearing the sharp breath he drew. After a while, he stopped her, pulling her up again. A heartbeat later, he was inside her, bringing her to fulfillment, delaying his own.

She pressed her forehead against his shoulder. "That was selfish of me. You didn't have your, um, moment of glory, I think you called it."

"Who says I'm done?"

"So, what are you waiting for?" She kissed him thoroughly, squeezing him rhythmically from deep inside, drawing a long moan from him.

"Ten years ago I could have stayed inside you and still been able to carry you to bed," he said, his tone of voice something between bragging and resignation.

"Can't do it anymore, huh?"

"I can try."

He leaned forward, then stood, holding her beneath her rear as she tightened her grip on him.

"For God's sake, don't laugh," he said. "It'll never work."

"I think you'd better hurry, 'cause one part of the process isn't cooperating very well."

They fell onto the bed. The laughter died. The pleasure escalated, peaked, exploded. Then contentment settled in.

"I'm sorry," she said after they'd rested awhile. Their faces were inches apart. "I never should have told you I was jealous. It's such a destructive emotion. I wish she hadn't died, Patrick. For your sake, I wish she hadn't died. I just wish I'd had a marriage, a love, like yours."

"Don't, Jasmine. You don't know anything about it."

"I know it had to have been rare. And perfect."

He couldn't handle another confession tonight. There would be time enough to tell her about Priscilla. Pulling her into his embrace, he closed his eyes and let sleep come.

Patrick needed to stretch but he didn't dare move. Jasmine slept curled like a kitten, her back pressed trustingly and peacefully against his chest and stomach, her hair caught beneath him. He needed time to think, time to sort everything out.

What if he'd gotten her pregnant?

It had seemed easy enough last night to accept the situation for what it was—fate and desire combining to provide them with one perfect night. In the bright light of day, however... He glanced toward the window. Correction, in the gray fog of morning, nothing seemed clear anymore.

What if he'd gotten her pregnant?

He'd be sixty-five when the child graduated from high school. If he lived that long. What the hell had he done? Taken away her choices? Saddled her with—

"Are you awake?" Jasmine asked, her legs moving against his, her voice husky with morning.

Damn. He hadn't finished working this out. Plus, their mutual secrets still clouded the air. "Yeah."

"Can you stop squeezing me?"

He relaxed his arm, which had tightened like a vise around her. He lifted up so that she could untrap her hair and roll over to face him as he moved back, as well. Two feet separated them. Neither touched.

Jasmine felt his regret, sad and palpable. She didn't want to put him on the spot. She didn't want him to feel any obligation toward her. She'd allowed herself the tiniest bit of hope last night—but that wasn't his fault. Love very often wasn't reciprocated.

She tucked the sheet tight against her throat. "This is a little awkward—"

A knock sounded at the front door. "That should be breakfast," he said, looking relieved as he threw the blankets aside and reached for his robe.

Jasmine dropped onto her back and stared at the ceiling. What had happened to the man who'd wooed her so tenaciously? She closed her eyes. A broken condom, that's what. He'd gone from being a man temporarily on leave from life to one with a potential lifelong obligation.

He stuck his head in the open door, a tray in his hands. "Do you want breakfast in bed or out here?"

"Out there, I guess." She just wanted to get dressed and go home.

Half a minute later he came into the room, a second robe hooked over his arm. He laid it on the end of the bed and walked toward the bathroom. "Food's hot."

Devastated, she stared at the matching blue garment. Last night he would have held the robe for her to slip into. He would have admired her. His eyes would have complimented her before, during and after. She swallowed the hot lump lodged in her throat. What had she done?

Cinching the belt, she walked into the living room. He'd set the tray on the coffee table in front of the fireplace, gray with the ashes of last night's fire. Her mouth twisted at the image that mirrored what had happened to their relationship during the night.

She poured coffee, giving herself something to do, then lifted the silver lids covering the plates. The omelets looked wonderful and nauseating. She heard the bathroom door open.

His hair was damp but combed, his face unshaved and appealing. She looked away as he sat beside her. How could something that had felt so right have gone so wrong?

"Aren't you hungry?" he asked, his voice softer than she'd ever heard it.

"Not really." She twisted one end of the belt with both hands. "I think maybe I should just leave."

"You're having regrets about last night."

"Aren't you?"

When he didn't answer her, she stood. "Okay," she said. "I got it."

He stopped her by grabbing her elbow, holding her still. "I have to tell you something."

"I don't need platitudes, Patrick. I've survived a lot worse in my life."

"My wife died twenty-five years ago."

Shocked, she turned to him as he stood beside her. She couldn't have heard him right. She shook her head.

"You assumed differently, I know. The lie was tied to withholding the truth about the heart attack. You thought I was still in mourning. I needed an excuse, any excuse, about why...things weren't working. Maybe it would help you to know that my father died of a massive coronary when he was my age. The idea that I was not invincible took some getting used to." He walked away from her, stopping to lean against the mantel. "As for Priscilla, my late wife, that's a different story. We intentionally got her pregnant when she was sixteen and I was seventeen so she wouldn't have to move out of state with her parents. A couple of years later I got her pregnant again, even though the doctor said it might kill her. And I would trade my life a hundred times over for the chance to go back and do things differently."

Hearing his self-recriminations, she ached for him, her heart expanding to allow some of his pain to seep into her, to relieve him of the whole burden.

"After Paige was born we found out Priscilla had a hole in her heart, a problem that would be identified today and fixed, but not always back then. During pregnancy, there is two or three times as much blood flow in the body, but at delivery there is a rapid shift back to normal. Her heart muscle was infected. It's a problem that can intensify with a second pregnancy. She was told to take it easy for a couple of years after Paige was born. We took precautions, but not enough. She got pregnant. When she was six months along, she lost the baby. 'An unfortunate accident,' the doctor called it," Patrick said bitterly, "unrelated to her heart condition, but once again the pregnancy took its toll. And after that, she just deteriorated. Her heart was permanently enlarged. She became pretty much an invalid. Fluid would build up in her lungs, requiring her to go into the hospital frequently for treatment. Each time, she got a little weaker, until shortly after Christmas when Paige was four, she died."

His words, at first dispassionate, became layered with grief.

"She died. And it was all my fault. I should have had a vasectomy. I should have stayed away from her." He drew a deep breath. "I lost her because I couldn't control myself. Her parents were right when they said I'd killed her. I had. And the best part of my life died with her. Then to add even more heartache, her family wouldn't have anything to do with Paige, so she grew up without grandparents after my father died two years later. It was just Paige and me, forever. I didn't even look twice at a woman for years and years. There was just my business and Paige. On top of everything, I was a lousy father."

His voice cracked on the last word and Jasmine wept—great, huge tears of sorrow for him, and Priscilla and

Paige, for herself and her children. The world was a cold, cruel, hard place to be, and some people lived with more pain than anyone should be asked to endure, especially when compounded with guilt.

"We all wish we could change our past," she said finally, wiping the tears from her face. "You can't blame yourself forever, Patrick."

He turned toward her. The lines in his face had deepened as he held his emotions in check. He wouldn't cry in front of her, she knew that much about him, no matter how much he suffered.

"I kept her alive for as long as I could in my mind, but the day came when she faded away. I couldn't see her face anymore. I couldn't hear her voice."

"I know," Jasmine whispered, truly knowing.

"About the time I'd thought maybe I'd like to get married again, Paige had grown up and she was so much like Priscilla that it hurt all over again. And Paige thought I needed her to be like her mother, for my sake, to please me somehow. She held everything inside her, when in fact she was more like me than her mother."

"But you have a good relationship with her now."

"We were close in a lot of ways then, because we worked together, but we never talked. Not about anything important." One side of his mouth quirked up a little. "And I tend to do things then tell people what I've done after the fact."

She forced a smile, grateful for the break in the tension. "No kidding."

"She didn't like that quality in me."

"I can't imagine why."

"She gives me hell now."

"Good for her."

"Rye's been good for her."

"Sometimes all it takes is the right person." She moved close to him. "I wish you'd trusted me enough before to tell me."

Patrick watched her edge nearer. She stretched out a hand to lay against his chest. The irony of her words struck him like a blow to the stomach. "How about you, Jasmine? You didn't trust me, either."

She frowned. Her hand dropped to her side. "You withheld your medical condition from me, which could have affected me, too. You let me think your wife had died recently, accepted my sympathy. I only withheld telling you about something that never even happened."

"I'm not talking about your plan to have a baby. What about the other secret you're keeping?"

She stared at him, realizing what he meant. "You looked in my file at Rye's house," she said.

"For that I apologize. But not for learning about your children and what had happened to you." He started to lay his hands on her shoulders but she jerked away. "Why didn't you tell me?"

The phone rang.

"Dammit." He scowled at the irritant then ignored it. "Why didn't you tell me?"

"Answer the phone, Patrick. It could be important."

Muttering a few curses, he snatched up the receiver and barked a greeting.

"Get up on the wrong side of the bed, boss?"

"This isn't a good time, Bill."

"If I had the slightest idea of your schedule I would have called at a better time. As it is—"

"I'll call you back."

"This is an emergency, Patrick. We've got big problems with the Russia contracts."

"Hell. What's wrong?"

Jasmine watched him settle into a chair, shifting gears, becoming—what had the newspaper article she'd finally

dug up with Rye and Paige's wedding announcement said
he was? President and CEO of O'Halloran Shipping? A
high-powered position. Status in his community. A man
who needed a wife to fill the proper role. A role she wasn't
destined to play.

Yet if she had conceived last night, he wouldn't aban-
don her. In fact, he'd probably force marriage. He faced
his responsibilities, whether or not they were his wishes.
But she'd seen too much regret in him this morning to believe it was what he wanted.

Thinking about it made her head hurt. She retreated into
the bedroom to pull on her clothes, all the while listening
to his end of the conversation.

"I don't know when I'll be back...Why don't you
choose, then? You'd know better than I would what qual-
ifications she needs...All right, all right. I can do that
much."

He was just hanging up the phone when she appeared,
dressed and ready to leave. He stared at her. His mouth
pulled into a taut line.

"I think we need some time apart," she said. "We've
given each other a lot to think about."

He steepled his fingers. "Why didn't you tell me about
your children?"

"Maybe it's time for you to go back to Boston, Patrick. It sounds like your company's in need of you."

He watched her intently, then pushed himself upright.
"If you want to go home, I'll take you."

"I'd rather walk."

He came toward her, stopping when her body tensed,
then inching closer. "What happened this morning, Night
Flower?"

"I don't know," she whispered. "I can't figure it out."

"Are you afraid, all of a sudden?"

"Of you? No, never."

"Of us," he amended. "Everything's been different since we woke up."

"I don't know what to tell you. Except that we've both been doing some growing lately, independent of each other. Maybe we're still on a journey."

He brushed the back of his hand down her face. She closed her eyes and shivered.

"It was wonderful, Patrick. All of it."

"Don't say that like it was the end."

"I don't mean to. It's just— Let's just give each other some time, okay?" She swallowed. "Go home. Catch up. Start living your life again, now that you have it back. If we have a problem to face later, we will. For now, though . . ." She couldn't get another word out.

He held her face in his hands and pressed his lips to hers. Jasmine threw her arms around his neck as she opened her mouth to him, needing him beyond words. *I love you, Patrick. I love you so much.* The words stayed trapped inside her, tightening around her heart painfully. *But I won't trap you.*

"I'll call you," he said, stepping back, not revealing anything in his expression.

She nodded and was gone.

A short, staccato knock sounded on Jasmine's apartment door hours later, startling her as she sat huddled on her couch, her arms wrapped around her tucked legs. She glanced at the clock. A little past noon. The knock sounded again. Still, she waited.

She watched as an envelope was shoved under the door, then listened until the footsteps disappeared. She forced herself off the couch.

Picking up the Express Mail packet she assumed had been signed for by her landlord, she returned to her seat and stared at it. From New Orleans. Probably from Monica, with word of Deacon's current whereabouts, she decided. She opened the envelope and tipped the contents onto the coffee table—a letter and— Oh, my God! A photograph of Matthew and Raine.

It had been taken from some distance, and they were looking at each other and laughing, so she could see only their profiles. But their blond hair shone in the sunlight, turning them into angels with brilliant halos. Matthew was taller than Raine by a good six inches so that she had to look up at him. Their smiles hadn't changed, otherwise they seemed so distant, so unlike the children she'd known. She clutched the flimsy print, holding it closer to her face, tears blocking her vision, then she pressed it to her heart as she lifted the letter to read, blinking her eyes several times to clear them.

She grabbed the telephone and dialed. Her legs bounced. "Be there, please. Be there," she prayed.

But the answering machine picked up on one ring and instructed her to leave a message.

"Rye, this is Jasmine. Monica sent the new address for Deacon. He's in London again." She gave the address breathlessly, her gaze returning to the photograph instantly. "Oh, God, Rye. I have a picture of my children. A picture taken last month. Monica took it secretly." Tears welled again. "Oh, they're so grown-up and so beautiful. Please, you have to go talk to him again. Please, Rye. These children—I don't know them. They'll never remember me if much more time goes by. He has to be tired of running."

She couldn't get her voice much above a whisper. "Please find them. Please. I'm so tired of being alone." With a little more volume, she added, "Call me as soon as you get this. 'Bye."

She didn't know when Rye would be back. Maybe not until it was too late again. She needed to know when he was expected back, and the only person she could ask was Patrick.

Pulling the telephone book from her desk drawer she looked up the number of his hotel and wrote it down. She stared at it for a long, long time, debating, then she closed the book.

She couldn't ask Patrick. He might take it upon himself to deal with the situation personally. She couldn't risk that, given his health. His father had died at Patrick's age.

Died. The phone book fell unheeded to the floor. She definitely couldn't ask him, not after what he'd survived. She couldn't live with herself if something happened to him because of her. No. She'd wait for Rye to call and let him do the job he was trained to do. Patrick had been given a second chance, which was more than she'd had. She wouldn't let him lose a minute of it.

Fourteen

———

Jasmine went about her daily routine at the Back Street Diner. As the early-morning waitresses finished up for the day, she and Star prepared for the lunch shift, cleaning and filling the ketchup and mustard bottles, dumping bags of prepared raw vegetables into servers so that salads could be made quickly and efficiently. She did everything by rote, without thinking about the task, including waving goodbye to the morning staff as they left.

It was Wednesday, her first day back at the diner since the night she'd spent with Patrick.

She looked up when the door opened, hating the hopeful leap of her heart, even as she knew he must have left town by now. In walked Gus, surprisingly smooth-shaven and decked out like the world's greatest Giants' fan—cap, sweatshirt, warm-up jacket. It drew her first smile in days.

He held out his arms as he turned a model's circle. "What d'you think, Miz Jazzy?"

"I think you look splendid."

"Splendid! That's a good word. Yep, I look splendid. Paddy bought it all for me." He took his usual seat at the counter. "I told him I could buy my own, but he wouldn't hear of it. No, sirree. Said I was his *guest.*"

She poured him a cup of coffee. "You had a good time, I gather."

"Hoo-eee! We had the best time. That Paddy, he knows baseball. Took me into that there clubhouse and introduced me 'round. Shook hands with Bobby Vanderkellen and Deadeye McGraff." He held up his hand and stared at it. "Haven't washed it since."

"Think it'll improve your own game?" she teased.

"Whoops! Almost forgot." Gus pulled an envelope from his back pocket. "He asked me to give you this."

She took the envelope addressed to her and stared at it, torn between ripping it open and ripping it up. She shoved it into her pocket instead as the door opened again. Rye Warner strode in and headed straight toward Jasmine, then took a seat next to Gus.

"You got my message," she said. Her stomach knotted with anticipation. "Oh, I'm so glad you're back."

"You look tired, Jazz."

She glanced at Gus, then back again. "I'm okay. If you can give me a couple of minutes, we can talk. Want some coffee while you wait?"

"Yeah, sure."

"I met your daddy-in-law," Gus announced.

Jasmine watched for Rye to react to that bit of news. He eyed the wizened old man, but his face revealed nothing. She'd always admired his coolness, wished for it at times.

"Did you?" he asked.

"Paddy and me, we're pals. Took me to the Giants' game Monday night. 'Course, he didn't take me home. Put me in a taxicab, give me a whole lot of money to pay the man, then off he went. Told me to take Abigail out someplace nice with the rest of the money."

"'Off he went'?" Rye repeated, angling toward Gus and focusing on the most important information being divulged.

"To the airport. Brought his valises with him and left 'em in the clubhouse during the game. Said he had to go on home."

Jasmine stood frozen. She felt Rye's gaze shift to her for a flickering moment.

"Did he say he'll be back?" Rye asked.

"That there's personal business. I 'spect you can ask him yourself. Did seem in an all-fired hurry, though. Had to take the red-eye, he called it."

Rye stared at Gus, then at Jasmine. "I'll take a seat in the booth over there," he said to her. "Come join me when you can take a breather."

Gus watched him go. "Man don't hold a candle to Paddy O'Halloran."

"Rye's a very good man, Gus."

"Mebbe. Who knows? Somethin' secretive about him, don't y'think?"

"I think your imagination's working overtime. Excuse me a minute, Gus. I really do need to talk to him."

She moved around the counter and slid into the booth at the far corner of the diner.

"About your message . . ." he began.

"Are you going to be able to go right away?" she asked.

"Jazz, you know the information isn't enough. It's the same as always. When there's something definite—"

"How much more definite can it get? We know his exact address. And now we have a current picture of the children. I figured you'd want copies of it, so I had a bunch made. I kept the original, though, because it's better quality." She pulled a print from her pocket and passed it to him.

After a few seconds of looking at it, he set it down. "When exactly did you get this?"

"Monday morning, first thing. I told you in my phone call." She leaned toward him. "You got my phone message, didn't you? That is why you're here?"

He took a sip of coffee. "Of course." Shifting in the seat, he picked up the photo again.

"So, now you're going to check it out, right?" she demanded.

"Definitely. I am definitely gonna check it out. Ah, along with the picture, did you get anything else?"

"You mean, aside from Deacon's address in London?"

"Yeah. Aside from that."

"Just a quick note from Monica saying she took the picture without anyone knowing. Deacon had brought the kids home for a week last month."

"Home to New Orleans?"

"To visit their grandparents. Why? Does that help?"

"It could. It's the first we've heard of them coming to the States. We might be able to check where they came from."

Jasmine squeezed his hand. "This is the most hope I've had in years, Rye. Tell me you feel that way, too."

"I told you when you hired me that I'd never make promises I didn't think I could keep, but that I'd look for your children as if they were my own. That hasn't changed."

She sat back, discouraged. "Meaning, I shouldn't get my hopes up."

"What about you and Patrick?" he asked, deftly changing the subject.

"Thanks for sending him my way."

"I didn't—"

She smiled. "Oh, yes, you did."

"So, things worked out okay between you?"

"We had some fun together." The letter in her pocket seemed to catch fire. She didn't know what it said, or how much to tell Rye. "He's unique."

"He has his own agenda," Rye concurred. "But I thought you might be able to change it."

"I wouldn't want to change him. I'm a little more realistic than that, Rye. We get past that needing-to-change-the-other-person stage at some point and hope to be accepted for who we are, not what someone wants us to be."

"He's a teller of convenient tales, I know. But you won't find a man with a bigger heart."

She knew that. She pinched the bridge of her nose, stopping tears before they started. "It's going to be difficult to look at Paige now," she said. "Or does she know?"

"Paige and I don't have secrets." He slapped a palm on the table. "I know you have to get back to work, and I need to get going on this business of yours. I'll keep in touch."

They stood simultaneously. She touched his arm. "Rye? Find my children, please."

"I'll do my best, Jazz."

She opened the envelope when he was out of sight. It wasn't a letter she could tie with a satin ribbon and keep forever in a memento box, but it was written in his hand and she would treasure it. He'd gone home to sort things out. He'd be in touch soon.

Why had that obstinate man finally decided to do what she asked?

"What's going on?" Patrick bellowed into the phone.

"It's a damn good thing at least one person knows how to locate you," Rye said in return. "Billie Jean wouldn't tell me where you are. What's the big secret?"

"Is Paige all right? Bill said it was an emergency."

"She's fine. This isn't about her. Where are you, Patrick?"

Patrick relaxed and sank into the nearest chair. "Home."

"You're making London your home these days?"

"How did you—"

"Dammit, man! What the hell do you think you're doing?"

"What you haven't been able to do for six years!" Patrick shouted back, then was greeted with dead silence.

"Not for lack of trying," Rye said finally, his voice considerably softer, and cooler.

"I'm sorry. I know from her file you've done—"

"Dammit! It was bad enough you intercepted a message intended for me—and erased it so I never even heard it—you invaded her privacy, as well. Those records are confidential."

He'd been lucky, that's all, Patrick thought. If he hadn't made his lawyer fax his new will to Rye and Paige's house, and if he hadn't had to delay leaving for Boston until after the Giants' game, he would have left hours before Jasmine's call had come in.

"You shouldn't have put temptation in my lap by leading me to her files," Patrick said.

"So this is *my* fault now? Uh-uh. I'll be there tomorrow. I want you on the first plane out of England. Swear on your daughter's life that you'll do it."

"I'm not swearing on anything. This is no longer your business. It's mine. I don't know why, but I have a feeling I can make him tell us where they are. Maybe I'm more motivated than you."

"Meaning what?"

"Meaning, I care about her differently than you do. You know, I've never considered myself self-centered—"

Rye snorted.

"But I've been self-focused all my life. I've had to be. My business wouldn't have survived, much less expanded to what it is today without that kind of singular focus. But I've discovered that the company is a poor substitute for happiness. I need to do this—for her, and for myself. I can't make it any worse, Rye. You haven't been able to get through to him. Maybe I can. Maybe I have more reason to.''

Rye sighed. ''The children have obviously been in a private school all these years, well hidden. We finally have a current photograph to go on. I can assign operatives from all over Europe to hunt. You could very well ruin the best chance we've had.''

''I have to try.''

''If you were fighting only Deacon, I'd give you better odds. But you're fighting the entire LeClerc family and everything that entails—the secrecy, the financial backing.''

''I know how it works. But I have to bring her children back,'' Patrick said to his son-in-law. ''She needs to forgive herself for losing her children, something she had no control over. But maybe it's something I can change.''

''I want a daily report,'' Rye said after a long pause. ''And if anything happens, you are to notify me immediately. Promise me, Patrick.''

''I'll notify you.''

''Immediately.''

Patrick sighed. After two full days of surveillance, combined with jet lag, he was exhausted. And even one of the finest hotels in London with all its creature comforts couldn't help him sleep better or longer. ''Immediately.''

''I saw her this morning.''

Alert, Patrick straightened. ''How is she?''

''She looks tired. Really tired. But she's full of hope.''

''I know. I heard it in her voice when she called you. Thanks for letting me do this.''

''Just be careful. Deacon has a lot to lose if he's cornered.''

''I'll be discreet. And I'll call you tomorrow. Give my daughter my love.''

''She sends hers. Take care, Patrick.''

Patrick cradled the phone, leaned back and closed his eyes. It felt good to take control again, to assume command of something, especially for Jasmine. He'd known from the beginning of their relationship that she held men in contempt. He didn't know whether or not he'd broken that barrier, with all that had happened between them, especially since she hadn't come to him when she needed help.

After he'd overheard her phone message to Rye, he'd gone back to the cottage, expecting to hear from her. Nothing. He'd waited hours and she hadn't called.

She didn't trust him. He had to prove he was trustworthy. And he had to prove to himself he was a whole man again, able to tackle the impossible, as he always had. He had to convince Deacon to bring her children back.

"Any word from Rye?" Maggie asked her sister days later as they left the locker room of the Carola, having finished work for the evening. "I've been afraid to ask."

Jasmine shook her head. J.D. pushed himself away from the wall he'd been leaning against and approached them. "I'm sure he would call me if he had any news," she said. "I wish I was there, though. It's so hard waiting."

"When he finds them," J.D. said, "you must let me talk with them. I'll help them understand. And forgive."

"Have you forgiven?" Jasmine asked.

"I've put it in the past."

"That's not the same thing, though, is it?"

"Perhaps not. But they'll need help. And not just from specialists who have learned from books rather than experience. I offer it with a full heart. You've been a good friend to me."

"What about me?" Maggie asked. "Aren't I your friend?"

They had moved out the front door together, coming to a stop as Maggie pulled her keys from her pocket and jangled them nervously. Jasmine watched them look at each other in silence. Finally, J.D. spoke.

"You and I will never be friends, Magnolia."

Even in the darkness, Jasmine could see her sister's face pale. "Well, I guess you put me in my place. I apologize for puttin' you on the spot." She hurried down the walkway. J.D. caught up with her.

"I cannot be friends with someone I want to take to my bed," he said, the words barely loud enough to carry to Jasmine.

"And I don't share a man with another woman," she flung back, tugging her arm from his grip. "Go see your precious Adrianna, why don't you. I'm sure she'd be much more understandin' than I am. And flexible."

She ran up the walkway and shoved the gate open. He followed until he knew she was safely in her car.

"Tactical error," Jasmine said, coming up beside him.

"She had to be told. She's been flirting. I don't want to get her hopes up."

"Chauvinist."

"Perhaps I am only looking out for her best interests."

"Why is it you men think you always know what's best for us?"

His brows lifted. "I think if I answer that honestly, I'll be beaten. But I get the feeling that you're not referring to me but to Patrick."

"Both of you. All of you. Men, in general."

"Have you not done the same, Jasmine? Discarded him before his emotions were fully engaged—to protect him?"

"And myself," she answered, ending the conversation, not saying out loud how very much she missed him. How at that moment she would have given up everything for him.

Patrick's confrontation with Deacon LeClerc had been building for the two frustrating, excruciating weeks he'd been in London. Daily, he dealt with the fact that Jasmine was afraid to care for him and Rye had no faith in his abilities. Paige had begged him to let the professionals handle it, his cardiologist had thrown a fit when he'd heard Patrick had flown out of the country, and Billie Jean had found a "wonderful replacement" for herself. The walls of his life were closing in around him. He had to scale them or tear them down, just as he always had. He couldn't sit on the ground waiting for them to squash him in the middle.

He needed to succeed because he needed her. It was that simple and that complicated.

The heat and humidity of London had been oppressive, matching his mood as day after day of constant surveillance of Jasmine's ex-husband had worn him down and revealed nothing of value. Deacon hadn't left the city. Occasionally he had dinner out with a woman he took to his flat afterward, always the same woman, who left early in the morning.

Ten minutes ago, Patrick had decided that Deacon knew he was being followed, and Patrick had finally forced the issue, his patience shattered. But like the rest of his life lately, it wasn't working out. He thought he'd had an ace in the hole. Once again, he'd been wrong. They'd taken each other's measure and Patrick had come up short. They'd argued and debated, accusing each other of real and imagined sins. Nothing Patrick said got through to him.

Now they stood, toe-to-toe and eye-to-eye, on the fringes of the bustling Leicester Square, people milling around them on the way to the half-price theater ticket booth, some staring, some ignoring the confrontation that Patrick was trying very hard to keep from getting violent.

"Get this through your head," Deacon said with a feral sneer. "They are *my* children. I have been looking out for them and providing for them all this time. They're happy, normal, well-adjusted adolescents who love and respect me. That won't change. You can send fifty private investigators to follow me—threaten me with jail like the other guy did—but you'll never find them."

"You won't be prosecuted. I guarantee that," Patrick said as Deacon stalked away.

He was gone, and Patrick stood staring until he was out of sight, a burning ache gathering in his chest and spreading like lighted gasoline through his body. He'd won. The bastard had won. And Patrick had just lost the biggest fight of his life.

Oh, he'd been so sure he could play the hero. Not only had he failed at that, he'd screwed things up even worse. He'd never failed so badly at something he had wanted so much. How the hell could he tell her what he'd done?

The ache intensified. He struggled to breathe. He felt blindly for the bench behind him and sat, hunching his shoulders. What was he going to do?

"Call off your dogs."

For a moment Jasmine thought it was another middle-of-the-night crank caller. She got them occasionally, a hazard of being listed in the phone book without a man's name attached. She glanced at the clock as she was about to hang up. Three-twenty.

"Did you hear me, Jasmine?" the commanding voice asked.

"Deacon?" she asked, disbelieving. She flung back the bed covers and sat up, brushing at her eyes. "Is that you?"

"I'm sick of being harassed. It stops here and now."

She shook—with anger, with fear, with a twinkling of hope that refused to die. "How are they?"

"They think to intimidate me with threats of jail and lifelong hatred from my children. I'm not intimida—"

"My children. How are my children?" An ache the size of California coiled around her, all-encompassing, oppressive.

"Thriving." The single, triumphant word was uttered with all the confidence of a man who had gotten everything he'd ever wanted in life.

"Do they ask about me?" She hated the weakness. She didn't want to beg, but she would have sold her soul at this point and never missed it.

"They think you're dead."

No! Oh, God, no. How could she fight that? Defeated, she sank to the floor, letting the bed support her back. "Why did you do it, Deacon? Why did you take them?"

Tension grew like a roller coaster car on its way up a long, steep hill. It crested with his harshly spoken words. "Because they loved you more."

The car dove down the track, instantly gathering speed and power. "That's not true!"

"Of course it's true. You made sure of that," he sneered into the loops and turns of her mind. "My mother saw it when she came to visit—how anxious the kids were to get home to you on Sunday nights. I was an outsider in my own home. You always stood between them and me."

"They loved us differently," she said, frantically trying to remember exactly. She should have known his mother would be the instigator of all of it. She'd hated Jasmine on sight, had never accepted her as her precious son's wife. And he'd been too spineless to stand up to his parents, for fear of being cut off from the family funds, which, in fact, had been a real possibility.

Stay calm, she told herself. She couldn't lose the only opportunity she'd been given in six years to plead her case. Controlling her emotions, she said, "I told Matthew and Raine that I loved them. They said it *back* to me, that's all. They were used to hearing it from me. Saying it was automatic. And they hugged me *back*. You wanted them to behave in the same way your parents had expected you to behave as a child. We had different approaches to parenting—we talked about that many times. But, Deacon, it doesn't mean they loved you less. Just differently.''

"Cut the games, Jasmine. I had enough from your new private eye. He tried the let's-reason-with-Deacon routine, too. Somebody needs to tell him he's too emotional for that kind of work.''

"What do you mean? I didn't hire someone new.''

"Then he sent someone in his place. I called the first one The Intimidator. Trust me, he'd be very hard to forget. This one used entirely different tactics. Patrick something. Ring any bells?''

Her head fell back against the bed; she squeezed her eyes shut. *Oh, Patrick. What have you done? How did you know?*

"You still there, Jasmine?''

"I'm here.'' Weary now, she simply waited.

"You really shouldn't pay him. He's strictly amateur, and to be honest, he didn't look all that healthy, either. Hey! I got it! Why didn't I see it before? He's your boyfriend, isn't he?''

She ignored his final question, which came echoed with laughter. "How did you change so much?'' she asked. "When we were married, I thought we had love and respect and friendship between us. You didn't care that I didn't come with a pedigree. Now I'm not fit to be the mother of your children? How can that happen? How did we get so lost from what we had?''

"We were never suited.''

His mother's voice was reflected clearly in those words. "We were, once. We still should have parted friends. Our children will always belong to both of us, even if I never see them again. You can't take that away from them or from me. They're in my soul and I'm in theirs. Please bring them home.'' She'd resorted to begging, after all, which was bound to make him feel more powerful. It didn't matter anymore.

"It's too late."

The phone line went dead. Her one and only opportunity to plead her case had gone to the judge and been dismissed before she'd barely entered her plea.

She dropped the phone, refusing to let even a moment of insecurity settle in. If he'd thought to douse whatever small amount of hope still flared within her, he hadn't succeeded. She would never give up the search. She would never give up hope. She would hound him all the way to hell, if necessary.

Straightening her spine, she turned on the bedside lamp and punched in a phone number with satisfying force. *Private* investigator Rye Warner was about to be awakened from a sound sleep. He had a whole lot of explaining to do. Especially letting Patrick risk his life.

Fifteen

Jasmine shut the door to the microwave and started the timer. She leaned against the counter a few seconds, stared at the scissors she'd placed there a few minutes earlier, then resolutely walked away from her tiny kitchen. She was killing time—consciously killing time. She couldn't remember feeling this much turmoil since the first months after Raine and Matthew had been stolen.

Patrick was missing.

She dropped onto the couch and put her head in her hands. Weariness battled pain. Guilt warred with need—selfish need. She wished she could take everything back, every announcement that they were from two different worlds, every order to go home, every demand for time to figure things out.

Her phone call to Rye had yielded that Patrick had been in London tracking Deacon for two weeks before confronting her ex-husband. He should have been home by now. Instead he'd disappeared. If anyone had heard from him in the past five days, they weren't admitting to it, including his secretary. It was as if the earth had opened up and swallowed him. If he walked through her door right now she didn't know whether she'd scream at him or faint with gratitude.

She pushed herself upright and began pacing her apartment—again. She wondered how many miles she'd logged in the past few days. If he was well and just hiding, she'd never forgive—

Someone knocked. She rushed to the door and swung it open. There he stood, looking uncharacteristically passive. A staggering range of emotions swept through her—shock, annoyance, relief. Anger. A huge red knot of anger that exploded from deep within her.

"Patrick O'Halloran, where have you been? What do you mean by putting your daughter and me through hell these past five days?" She stood back, holding the door open for him, making a violent gesture that vaguely resembled an invitation into the room. Silently, he picked up his luggage and went inside. She slammed the door behind him, a picture-rocking, wall-vibrating, self-satisfying slam.

Patrick glanced around the neat, homey living room and kitchen, avoiding her gaze, knowing she stood with her arms crossed and foot tapping.

"Well?" she said at last, exasperated.

"I can explain every—"

"Are you well?"

"I'm fine."

"Have you been in some hospital somewhere, not telling us *for our own good* again?"

"No." It wasn't quite the truth. He'd gone to the hospital but had been diagnosed only with a stress reaction, which had affected his blood pressure, but not his heart. However, Jasmine was beyond mad, and he didn't want to add to that now. To think he'd once thought of her as soothing and gentle. "I'm sorry."

She spread her arms wide. "Sorry? You're *sorry?* Well, how very manly of you to apologize." She marched up to him. "Do you have any idea how many people have been looking for you? Did it even once occur to you to call the people who care about you and tell them you're all right? By the way, your daughter finally knows you had a heart attack, because I told her. I couldn't believe you hadn't."

"I was going to."

She threw her hands in the air. "When hell froze over? Or perhaps on the twelfth of never? When are you going to get it through that thick skull of yours that none of us has to be protected?"

"I got it, all right? I got it!" he shouted. Her chin came up; her eyes fired daggers at him. He closed his eyes and drew a deep breath. She'd been worried, he realized. "I'm not arguing with you," he said more softly.

"Why not? I need to fight right now." She started shaking. "Because if I don't fight I'm going to cry. Aw, what the hell. I guess I'll just cry anyway. You'd better hold me."

He barely had time to catch her when she threw herself at him.

"I was so scared," she said, her arms clamped around him.

Guilt swamped him. He didn't deserve her concern. Still, he held her, because he needed it, too.

"I've done something horrible," he said when she quieted at last. "Maybe unforgivable. But I have to tell you, because I promised myself I'd never keep anything secret from you again."

"Wait a second," she said, moving away to wipe her eyes and blow her nose.

The tension was almost unbearable for him. He needed to get this over with. Now. Amazed, he watched as she lifted the phone and dialed.

"He's here," she said into the receiver.

He could hear his daughter screaming from where he stood eight feet away.

"*I* get first crack at him," Jasmine said. "He'll be over later. What's left of him when I'm done, that is." She nodded to whatever Paige said, then hung up. The microwave beeped four times. She looked in that direction, even took a step that way, then instead motioned for him to sit on the sofa with her.

"Do you need to get something out of the oven?" he asked.

"It's nothing. Tell me what horrible thing you've done." Jasmine watched him sit carefully on the couch. Her nerves had settled into jitters that she tried to hide. He was safe. He was well. He was here. She knew what he had to tell her. She could make it easy for him or she could make it difficult. She had to decide in a hurry.

He faced her, not shirking any responsibility. "I intercepted your telephone message to Rye with Deacon's address. I went to England and confronted him."

She made it easy. "I know."

Tension drained from him in one long, surprised exhale. "You do?"

"Deacon called me."

"I shouldn't have interfered," he said. "I thought I could convince him. I thought I had advantages that Rye didn't have. I was wrong. And now I've cost you all hope."

"Nothing can kill my hope. You did something good, Patrick. I got to ask him why he did it. I'd never known why. Now I do. If you hadn't said whatever it was you said to make him mad enough to call, I never would have known. Not that I wasn't furious with you at first—and

Rye, as well, for keeping it from me. Then you disappeared...."

"I had a lot to work through," he said. "I know it's no excuse, but it's the truth."

She rested her head against his arm. "Deacon told me they think I'm dead."

"God."

She felt him shudder. "Shh. It's all right. I've thought about it. It would have been worse if they'd thought I'd abandoned them. I'll find them. Someday. Somehow. We're tied by our heartstrings. Nothing can cut them altogether."

"He told me they have new identities, but I don't believe him," he said. "His name means too much to him. When they're adults, he won't be able to hide them. We—*you'll* be able to track them down."

"You got to him, Patrick, in a way that Rye never did."

"I tried to appeal to him as one father to another. I told him about J.D. I told him about Paige, how I'd never given her a mother, how hard it had been for her. I thought if he knew, it would make a difference. *The* difference."

"But you didn't know that he doesn't have paternal instincts like you. He just needs to possess."

"I wanted to be your hero," he admitted softly.

Jasmine slid her arm under his and leaned more heavily against him, cherishing his words, words that made everything else she had to say and do easy. She tried to let the past find its place in her heart and mind. She had to let go. She'd already figured that out. It wouldn't stop her from searching, but she had to put it where it belonged.

"I need your help with something," she said.

"Anything."

She pushed away from him and stood. "Before you knocked on my door, I was in the process of doing something. If you could help, I'd appreciate it."

"Of course. What?"

She walked to the kitchen counter bar that served as a dining table and picked up the pair of scissors resting there. Returning, she handed them to Patrick, then turned around, not wanting to see the look on his face. "Cut off my braid."

For a full fifteen seconds he stood silently behind her. She needed him to do this, to end her mourning. To throw off her sackcloth and ashes.

"Why didn't you tell me about your children?" he asked in a near whisper. "Did you really trust me so little?"

Jasmine turned and pressed her hands to his face. "I think I trusted you from the minute we met. I was just so used to counting on only myself that I wouldn't let you in. I'm sorry for that, Patrick. I really am." She folded her arms over her stomach. "But every time I talked about them, I lost a little bit of them. I needed to remember the way they looked and sounded. Even their scent stayed with me a long time. Then they started fading and I could hardly remember anymore. Now... now I have this new photograph of them, something I always thought I wanted to have. But these children are strangers to me. Complete strangers. It's put distance between us that I never wanted. But it's real, and I have to face it." She spun around, then grabbed her braid at her nape. "Cut it right below my hand. Do it, Patrick. Please, just do it."

The sound reverberated in her head like a chain saw cutting through a centuries-old redwood. Then suddenly the weight was gone and hair fell against her cheeks, sticking to the tears that were as much relief as agony. She turned and saw pain reflected in his eyes, and her hair clenched in his hand. She didn't know what to do with it. She closed her fists.

Patrick saw the emotions laid bare on her face. The braid dangled from his hand like a useless appendage. He understood why she needed to cut it; he just wished he hadn't been the one to do it. Would she cut him out, too?

Knowing he had to handle the last detail, he sought his suitcase, opened it and laid the braid inside. He returned to her side.

"Thank you. I couldn't have." Her words were stilted and quavery.

He watched her search for and find some peace. "You look different," he said.

"I'll get it evened up tomorrow. It'll be okay. I have one more favor to ask, Patrick." She moved closer. "Make love to m—"

Patrick kissed her before she'd finished the sentence, relief running through his mind in a blinding flash of light. She didn't blame him. She didn't hate him. She even wanted him still. The sounds of need she made drew his own fire, and he lifted her into his arms. Spotting an open door, he headed there, then stood her beside the bed with its handmade quilt. She moved a teddy bear and a baby doll onto the night table, and he knew without her saying that they had belonged to her children.

They worked at buttons and zippers and elastic and hooks until they were free of clothing and fell across the bed. Their mouths attacked and savored; their tongues invited and sought. He dragged his lips down her to one thrusting breast and pebbled crest then to the other, tasting, measuring, arousing, luxuriating. She tasted like heaven itself. Without her, life would be pure hell.

He glided a hand down her body, into the soft curls now damp and heated. She responded to his inquisitive touch as his fingers stroked and separated and pressed, sending her hips off the bed and drawing a gasp of pleasure. She wrapped a hand around his masculine heat, driving him wild. Flattening her against the bed, he moved above her, kissing her as he went.

"Hurry," she pleaded against his lips then released a long, slow moan as he sheathed himself in her inviting warmth.

He'd come home. Did she feel it, too?

The rhythm started powerfully and stayed there without apology, a driving, pounding cadence that asked and answered. Teased and satisfied. Claimed and yielded. She dug her fingers into his back as she lifted her hips higher against him, the friction driving him wild. He couldn't wait a second longer. But he had to . . . had to, for her sake. He tried to make a blank of his mind, but the sensations engulfing him couldn't be ignored.

"Oh, sugar," she said at last, her body growing taut, her fingers digging deeper.

"I love you, Jasmine," he said as she climaxed, and he felt her reaction to his words in the further tightening of her muscles and the hoarse sounds from her throat, sounds he matched with unrestricted cries of his own as he made her his, for a lifetime, he hoped.

He didn't give himself time to relish the feeling of completion. He pulled back just a little and looked at her. She smiled, and his world was complete. "Marry me, Night Flower. I know I'm not much of a bargain. I don't come with any guarantees except one—that I'll spend the rest of my life loving you."

She started to answer. He cut her off.

"A lot has happened to me in a couple of months. It's made me look at how I want to live the last half of my life. My secretary is retiring and I couldn't face breaking in a new one, so in the last few days I've worked out a deal with my partners so that I don't have to work full-time in Boston. We can live here. I'll have to go back East once a month for a while, but eventually I'll just be a silent partner. Or maybe I'll start up a branch office here. It doesn't matter."

She opened her mouth. He stepped over her response.

"We can live as simply as you'd like, be as social as you're comfortable with. And whatever other objections you have, I'll find solutions for them, too."

"Yes." The simplicity of the single word made her heart dance. "Yes," she said a little more emphatically when he didn't react. She brushed his hair with shaking fingers. "I love you, Patrick. I've loved you for a long time. I wasn't ready for a second chance before, but now I am. You did that for me. You made me believe that anything is possible, that it's never too late."

She reveled in the tenderness of his kiss, enjoyed his strength as he enveloped her with warmth and gratitude.

"Let's find out if we made a baby," she said. She bounced up, retrieved a robe from the back of her bedroom door, and slid into it, then scooped his pants off the floor and tossed them at him.

"How can we do that?" He sat on the edge of the bed and pulled them on.

"The miracles of modern science, of course. Cutting my hair wasn't the only item on my agenda when you showed up. I had a sequence, you see. Take a few pregnancy tests, shut them in the microwave where I wouldn't be tempted to look at them until the timer went off, cut my hair, then see if we got lucky."

He reached for her hand as he stood, then he looked into her eyes, brimming with love. "Even without knowing whether we'd see each other again, you counted being pregnant with my baby as lucky?"

"Patrick, there's one indisputable fact I've learned about you. Whatever else happens in your life, you feel your responsibilities clear to your bones. You wouldn't have left me to go through this alone."

"The baby would be mine, too."

"I wouldn't have kept it from you, if that's what you're thinking. That would have made me no better than Deacon." She drew a deep breath. "Well, are you ready to find out?"

"Ready." He followed her into the kitchen. When she opened the microwave door he could see three different kinds of tests.

"You don't have a whole lot of *faith* in the miracles of modern science, however," he said with a grin.

"I heard they're not completely accurate. I figured if all three said yes or no, I could believe it."

He looked over her shoulder as she examined each one and compared them to the instructions on the boxes. He swallowed once. Twice. He forced air into his lungs. She turned to him, holding up the last test.

"Yes. Yes. Yes."

"Oh, God. Jasmine." She'd taken his breath away. He was going to be a father again. A better one, this time, with Jasmine's help. Tears welled in her eyes as he watched. "We made a baby."

"Yes." Her voice shook with surprise and happiness. "Second chances, Patrick. We've been given the best one of all."

He pulled her into his arms and squeezed her until she complained, then he loosened his hold and she nuzzled his chest and sniffled. He started to laugh.

"What's so funny?" she asked.

"I *have* to get married for the second time in my life."

"Nobody's forcing you, sugar."

He laughed harder at the dryly spoken words. "Seventeen and forty-seven. What are the odds?"

"As long as you're just as happy this time around."

He thought about it for a moment. "Happier. I know I can provide for us. I know what I'll do differently as a father this time. And as a husband."

"All you have to do is love us, Patrick. Everything else is gravy."

"I love you," he said as he bent to kiss her. "With all my battered heart. That won't ever change."

She pressed a hand to her chest then to his. "And I give you my beating heart to keep with yours, so that if yours ever falters, mine will keep you alive, just as my love lives in you now and always."

He kissed her tenderly, to celebrate the moment . . . and passionately, to celebrate their future . . . and endlessly, to celebrate their love. It was a kiss for all time.

Epilogue

Patrick watched his wife move gracefully across the room, the one box she wasn't trusting to the movers held securely in her arms. She set it by the front door, next to her purse. Any minute now they would be invaded by a small army of oversize men who would pack everything else into boxes and carry them off to their new home two miles away.

He was going to miss this cozy little place where their marriage had taken root. In the two months since their wedding, they'd honeymooned at a friend's cabin in the Rockies, then had alternated time between Boston and here. He preferred here.

He watched her stretch the kinks out of her back, his gaze tracing the curves of her body, a body he knew better than his own. She wasn't far enough along in her pregnancy to show yet, except in her breasts. He wasn't complaining. He only had to look at her or think about her— or smell her shampoo—to feel desire.

Her hair swung against her cheeks as she turned and caught him staring at her, wanting her, needing her. He didn't hide anything from her anymore.

"The movers will be here any second," she said with a wicked grin, teasing him with the knowledge he'd have to wait.

He took the few steps necessary to reach her side. "Where's your spirit of adventure?"

"In my new home." But she gave him a promise in a kiss that lit his fire spontaneously.

A knock sounded. He groaned and backed away. "I'd better go into the bedroom for a second," he said, "and make myself presentable."

She chuckled as she headed to the door and opened it.

"Oh, my God!"

Her voice held the highest pitch he'd ever heard, the most tension, the most shock. He turned and saw Deacon, and her children, standing in the doorway. He reached her side as she wavered, held her until she could throw her arms around her children, sobbing, trying to talk at the same time, telling them how beautiful they were.

Matthew was taller than Jasmine by several inches, Raine, as tall as her mother. All three had the same white-blond hair, although Raine's curled beguilingly down her back.

Patrick looked at Deacon.

"I'm prepared for whatever consequences you settle on, legal or personal," he said, obviously shaken. "I can't live with the lies any longer. I waited until their school year was over, then I told them everything. Right now they hate me a lot. Maybe they won't ever forgive me. But the things you said and the things that Jasmine said finally convinced me I couldn't continue this charade." He looked at Jasmine and their children as they huddled together. "I'll leave them with you. If and when they want to see me, I hope you'll let me know."

He turned away.

"Deacon," Jasmine said, clutching her children to her side.

He faced her and straightened his shoulders.

"Thank you."

He nodded then left, shutting the door behind him.

"We never forgot you, Mom," Matthew said, his voice cracking. "Rainey and I reminded each other all the time about you."

"I remembered the cookies," Raine said. "And the bedtime stories. Matthew remembered the trips to the park and being pushed on the swing. Dad did a horrible thing. He's a horrible, horrible man."

"He did do a horrible thing," Jasmine said. "But he's trying to make up for it. We'll just take some time together and see what happens, okay?"

With her arms around them, she smiled through her tears at Patrick as she introduced them, and he saw a flicker of jealousy cross their faces. They'd probably expected to be alone with her. Well, he'd expected that for himself, too, but he was more than willing to adapt. It would just be another adventure during this second half of his life. Nothing of consequence ever came easy.

A moment of pure selfishness drifted through him, gratitude that she was already pregnant, because if her children had come home to her before the pregnancy, it might never have happened. There would be adjustments for all of them, but they would work together, as a family. A family for always.

*   *   *   *   *

SILHOUETTE

Desire

COMING NEXT MONTH

YOU'RE WHAT?! Anne Eames

Bachelors & Babies

Michelle Purdue longed for a baby, so she went to a sperm bank. But then she shared a night of passion with Kevin Singleton! When he learned Michelle was pregnant, Kevin was convinced that the baby couldn't be his, but then he caught the baby fever himself!

SURRENDER Metsy Hingle

Aimee Lawrence had found Mr Right—but he insisted she sign a prenuptial agreement! Now he had to prove his feelings for her ran much deeper than lust...

THE TEMPORARY GROOM Joan Johnston

Man of the Month

When rancher Billy Stonecreek married Cherry Whitelaw, he had only wanted a mother for his twin daughters. But it didn't take long before he was falling for his fiery bride!

MICHAEL'S BABY Cathie Linz

Three Weddings and a Gift

When a baby was left on the doorstep, Brett Munro and Michael Janos found themselves playing proud newlywed parents. But could this baby turn their practical marriage into a love match?

THE BRIDE'S CHOICE Sara Orwig

Caleb Duncan and Juliana Aldrich had to marry to claim an inheritance. Could Juliana's three orphaned nephews convince the hesitant couple to make a lifetime commitment out of a temporary marriage.

REGAN'S PRIDE Diana Palmer

Texan Lovers

Coreen Tarleton knew she had made an impression on Ted Regan—but he had pulled himself away from her loving arms. Years later, Coreen was back, determined that the Texan's pride wouldn't get in their way again...

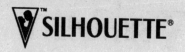

™ SILHOUETTE®

Treat yourself to...

Wanted:
Mother

*Silhouette's annual tribute to motherhood takes
a new twist in '97 as three sexy single men
prepare for fatherhood and saying "I Do!"*

Written by three captivating authors:

Annette Broadrick
Ginna Gray
Raye Morgan

Available: February 1997   Price: £4.99

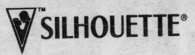

Spring is in the air with our sparkling collection
from Silhouette...

SPRING
fever

Three sexy, single men are about to find the love
of a lifetime!

Grace And The Law by Dixie Browning
Lighfoot And Loving by Cait London
Out Of The Dark by Pepper Adams

Three delightful stories...one romantic season!

Available: March 1997   Price: £4.99

FREE!

FOUR FREE
specially selected
Desire ® novels
PLUS a Mystery Gift
when you return this card...

Return this coupon and we'll send you 4 Silhouette Desire® novels and a mystery gift absolutely FREE! We'll even pay the postage and packing for you.

We're making you this offer to introduce you to the benefits of the Reader Service™– FREE home delivery of brand-new Silhouette novels, at least a month before they are available in the shops, FREE gifts and a monthly Newsletter packed with information.

Accepting these FREE books and gift places you under no obligation to buy—you may cancel at any time, even after receiving just your free shipment. Simply complete the coupon below and send it to:

THE READER SERVICE, FREEPOST, CROYDON, SURREY, CR9 3WZ.

EIRE READERS PLEASE SEND COUPON TO: P.O. BOX 4546, DUBLIN 24.

NO STAMP NEEDED

Yes, please send me 4 free Silhouette Desire novels and a mystery gift. I understand that unless you hear from me, I will receive 6 superb new titles every month for just £2.30* each, postage and packing free. I am under no obligation to purchase any books and I may cancel or suspend my subscription at any time, but the free books and gift will be mine to keep in any case. (I am over 18 years of age)

D6XE

Ms/Mrs/Miss/Mr _____
BLOCK CAPS PLEASE

Address _____

_____

_____ Postcode _____

COMING NEXT MONTH FROM

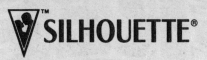 SILHOUETTE®

Sensation

A thrilling mix of passion, adventure and drama

DRIVEN TO DISTRACTION Judith Duncan
MACKENZIE'S PLEASURE Linda Howard
MICHAEL'S HOUSE Pat Warren
UNBROKEN VOWS Frances Williams

Intrigue

Danger, deception and desire

THE CHARMER Leona Karr
LOVE VS. ILLUSION M.J. Rodgers
BELLADONNA Jenna Ryan
MYSTERY BABY Dani Sinclair

Special Edition

Satisfying romances packed with emotion

ON MOTHER'S DAY Andrea Edwards
A COWBOY IS FOREVER Shirley Lawson
THE CASE OF THE BORROWED BRIDE
Victoria Pade
THE FATHER OF HER CHILD Joan Elliott Pickart
THE WOLF AND THE WOMAN'S TOUCH
Ingrid Weaver
**THE RANCHER AND HIS UNEXPECTED
DAUGHTER** Sherryl Woods